LAZA

LAZARUS

Alain Absire

Translated by Barbara Bray

faber and faber

LONDON · BOSTON

First published in 1985
by Editions Calmann-Lévy, Paris
as *Lazare, ou Le grand sommeil*
First published in the USA in 1988
by Harcourt Brace Jovanovich, Inc., Florida
First published in Great Britain in 1988
by Faber and Faber Limited
3 Queen Square London WC1N 3AU

Printed in Great Britain by
Redwood Burn Limited, Trowbridge, Wiltshire

British Library Cataloguing in Publication Data

Absire, Alain
Lazarus.
I. Title
843'.914[F]

ISBN 0–571–14530–2

ONE

Lazarus ben Chaim, carpenter and cabinetmaker, was a person of some importance in the village of Bethany, near Jerusalem. Every day, Eliphas, his apprentice, could be seen going up the village street to his workshop, laden with heavy beams. People went to Lazarus to order a chest, a table, or a stool, to ask him to put up an arbor along a wall, to mend the beam or colter of a plow. He supplied masons with doorposts and lintels. Women bought bushels from him for measuring corn, frames for pallet beds, bins, kneading troughs. He never stopped working except to honor the Sabbath. He lived with his two sisters, Martha and Mary, and with Susannah, his young wife, barely fifteen, whom he loved dearly. By turns woodcutter, joiner, wheelwright, builder, and maker of yokes and plows, he was one of the richest men in Bethany. Everyone respected and admired him.

Then, that winter, Lazarus fell ill.

Violent coughing soon tore his chest to pieces. His forehead burned, and the air seemed to stick in his throat. Unable to walk or even stand, he who never left his shop until nightfall now had to give up working. The doctor prescribed great quantities of honey. Susannah and his sisters prayed day after day for his recovery. But he only got worse. When he began to choke, Martha sent Eliphas to find the Galilean—also a carpenter—who one autumn night had taken refuge in their house from men who sought to kill him. Didn't people say that last Sabbath, at the Pool of Siloam, this strange man, half magician, had restored the sight of a man blind from birth?

But unfortunately the Galilean was on the other side of the Jordan and would not come. All he said, in one of his typically obscure statements, was, "This sickness is for the glory of God, that the Son of God might be glorified thereby." Eliphas returned to Bethany alone, and two days later, at the ninth hour, Lazarus died.

As soon as his raucous breathing stopped and his hands no longer clutched the blanket, the three women standing vigil realized he had entered the "Great Sleep."

Mary, on the other side of the room, began to wail. "Why didn't the Galilean come?" she cried. "We took him in and hid him. We ran a great risk for him. He restores sight to the blind—he could have cured our brother if he'd wanted to!"

Martha said nothing, but gently passed her hand over Lazarus's open eyes, closing the lifeless lids. She took a cloth and wiped away the sweat that made his hair stick to his forehead. She drew the blanket up over his bare unmoving chest. He slept now, his head on the alabaster neck rest.

Susannah went over to the bed. Her cheeks were still dry: she was unable to weep. All she could do was kneel by the dead man, cover his cheeks with kisses, and murmur, "Wake, wake. . . ."

Martha went over to Mary, who was still wailing, and put her arms around her. "I suspect it was impossible for the Galilean to come back to Jerusalem," she said quietly. "He would have been arrested and stoned to death."

At the eleventh hour, as the winter night fell and the house grew cold again, Martha undressed her brother's still-warm body, to wash it. Susannah, as in a dream, poured fragrant oil on her beloved husband's hair and rubbed his stiffened limbs with nard, myrrh, and sweet-smelling aloes. With Eliphas's help, they wrapped the corpse in a white shroud, wound narrow strips of linen around the hands and feet, and covered the head with a cloth, which they fastened around the neck in a kind of bag. Then they carried the body up the outside staircase and into the upper room, laid it on the bed, and, collecting all the lamps in the house, arranged them around the body on metal or earthenware stands. Because of the cold, they lighted the charcoal brazier. With Mary, who had not stopped weeping, they put on their oldest *saq*s, dirty and made of rough material, and went to fetch the people of Bethany, their relatives and friends, so they could pay their respects to the deceased.

Many men and women came back with them, even though it was night, for they all loved Lazarus. The upper room was filled with people praying.

5

For hours Susannah, stunned with grief, remained in the background, sitting in a dark corner and staring at the shrouded body. In the flickering yellow light of the oil lamps it looked surprisingly long and tall. She saw the same images, over and over again, of Lazarus in the autumn, two years ago. He was dressed in his holiday best, coming to fetch her from her father's house at the other end of Bethany. She was waiting for him outside the door: it was the eve of their marriage. A procession formed around them. She lay down in a litter and was carried to Lazarus's house. Her face was veiled and her brow hung with jewels and thin ornaments of gold. The crowd sang the traditional wedding songs. There was dancing, games, trials of skill. "Behold, thou art fair, my love," Lazarus had sung, "behold, thou art fair. Thy hair is as a flock of goats that appears from Mount Gilead. Thy teeth are like white sheep newly washed. Thy lips are a thread of scarlet."

The festivities grew merrier, noisier, but when evening came, the young couple withdrew and went up together to this same upper room, to caress and make love on the same bed where he lay today. How could she forget the softness of his beard and long scented hair, the smell of rosemary and marjoram on his skin, the roughness of his carpenter's fingers and palms? So, while Martha and Mary gave voice to their grief by their brother's motionless body, Susannah sat apart all night silently, her head full of memories.

The funeral procession set out at the second hour next morning. The *qadim*, or east wind, was blowing, and the sky above the village was clear. Eliphas and Samuel carried the bier, helped by Judas the potter and Joad the sandalmaker. Susannah, Martha, and Mary, dressed in their *saq*s, their heads covered with tattered old shawls, walked a few paces

6

ahead. The two sisters wailed and threw dust over their faces, but Susannah hid her face and was silent. Such restraint, contrary to custom, amazed the people of Bethany standing along the road to watch the procession go by, and some concluded that she had not loved Lazarus as much as they supposed. Four professional mourning women followed the dead man as he lay wrapped in his shroud, hands and feet bandaged, face covered by the cloth knotted at his neck. Their cries often drowned out the mournful sounds the musicians drew from their flutes.

When they reached the burial place, a stone wall with openings in it, the four bearers stooped at the narrow entrance, then went down the uneven steps hewn in the rock. Bent double, they made their way into a small cave that served as the burial chamber. Joad lighted a lamp, and they laid the body, stiff and straight, on a ledge carved out of the rock. Then they quickly emerged to let the three women enter. Martha and Mary arranged the pots and jars of spices around the dead man. When Mary threw herself facedown on the ground, Susannah, now in tears, drew back and stood apart, as she had done all night in the upper room. She felt herself sweating despite the cold. The shrill cries and the sound of flutes outside suddenly seemed unbearable. In the semidarkness she could clearly make out the lines of her husband's body beneath its coverings: his long legs, the bulge of the knees, the slight fold made by his arms tied to his sides, the wide, powerful shoulders. She could see the curve of the shroud over his mighty chest, the hollows around his eyes, the shape of his nose. Gazing at the crease in the cloth where his mouth was, she thought for a moment that he might still be breathing. . . . What madness! And yet she could not believe life had

7

forsaken that strong young body, or that the warm skin she had so often stroked was now dry and chill. She couldn't breathe, and had to lean against the wall to keep from falling.

"O Lord," cried Martha, near her, "who sees and understands all, hear my prayer! Send Gabriel the messenger of light, and Michael the chief of your angels, with all his hosts, that they may go with the soul of my brother Lazarus and bring him to your presence!"

When the women left the tomb, Eliphas removed the wooden wedge that held the heavy boulder, round as a millstone, in place. And the stone rolled into the deep groove carved in the ground, and closed up the entrance to the tomb.

Then they all went back to the house, to drink wine and eat the bread of mourning at the funeral banquet.

Four days went by. Many Jews, some from Jerusalem, came to see Martha, Mary, and Susannah, and tried in vain to console them.

The young widow never left the upper room. She spent hours talking to Mary about Lazarus and praying for him. She had stopped eating: her only interest was remembering the man she had loved.

On the morning of the fifth day, Martha, as she was grinding corn, noticed a group of about twenty people coming toward the house. She recognized the carpenter-magician and the big man with the goatee who accompanied him everywhere. She ran to the carpenter.

"If you'd been here," she cried, "my brother wouldn't have died! I know you heal the blind, and I sent for you. Why didn't you come?"

The Galilean looked at her. She saw his small, deep-set brown eyes, low forehead, long hooked nose, light beard, and thick lips. His cloak was made of two grubby blankets sewn together. His dusty hair fell loose on either side of his face, not in the two braids prescribed by the Law.

This man is nothing but a beggar, she thought.

"Do not reproach me," he said in that absurd Galilean accent of his. "Your brother will rise again."

"Yes," she answered in anger. "At the resurrection, on the last day."

"I am the resurrection, and the life," he said. "He that believes in me, though he were dead, yet shall he live."

How dared he utter such words? Only the Almighty could bring Lazarus back to life. Did he take himself for God's equal? The very fact that he hadn't come sooner showed he had no power. That story about the blind man at the Pool of Siloam was a hoax. She looked at the bunch he had with him: a beggar, a man with only one leg, a few other cripples. . . . Why do you follow him? she felt like shouting at them. He's a liar, a blasphemer, he can't perform miracles, and the people of Jerusalem are right to want to kill him.

"Whoever believes in me shall never die," he said. "Do you believe in me, Martha?"

Why did he ask this question? He looked at her fixedly, as if to read her thoughts. The big man with the goatee was looking at her, too. She turned away. None of those who'd come with him protested. Weren't they shocked by his words? But he seemed so sure of himself that suddenly, despite her anger, she hesitated.

She remembered the long autumn evening he came to take refuge in their house, because Lazarus was a carpenter like

9

himself. They had shared bread, dried fish, and wine. "I am the light of the world," he had said when the meal was over. "He that follows me shall not walk in darkness."

And for reasons she could not now explain, she had believed in his strength and power. As had Lazarus, for he had often spoken of that strange night.

"Do you believe in me, Martha?" he asked again, softly.

"I believe in you," she answered, lowering her eyes, not sure whether she was lying or telling the truth.

When he heard her reply, the Galilean turned to those who were with him and said: "My friend Lazarus is dead. He offered me shelter in his house when certain people, because of my words and deeds, would have killed me. I am glad I was not here when he died, so that now you may believe in me."

Then he turned again to Martha and said, "Go fetch your people and take me to the place where you have laid him."

When they came to the cave where Lazarus lay, the Galilean told the big man with the goatee to remove the stone that guarded the entrance.

"But he has been dead five days," protested Susannah, who was also there, with Mary and some friends from the village.

"Believe in me," said the Galilean, "and you will see the glory of God."

The big man slipped off his cloak and took hold of the stone with his enormous hands. He braced his legs; the muscles stood out on his arms. Slowly the stone rolled aside along the groove in the rock.

Hearing what was happening, Judas, Joad, and other people from Bethany came running. Martha saw that more than fifty onlookers now stood by the open tomb. They were all staring at the dark, narrow passage that led down five or six steps to the funeral chamber.

The Galilean covered his bowed head with his cloak, lifted his hands to heaven, and began to pray. "Father," he said, "hear my prayer and bring Lazarus forth from Abraham's bosom, that you may be glorified in the Son." Then for a long while he was silent.

When nothing happened, some people began to murmur, asking who he thought he was and how he dared claim he could bring the dead back to life. But no one moved. Despite their incredulity or indignation, they waited.

No magician has such power, Susannah was thinking. He is crazy to pretend that he can do such a thing. Once again her eyes blurred with tears. She should never have come here with Martha this morning; it was only adding to her suffering.

The waiting continued. The Galilean lowered his arms, but still stood silent, his head bowed and covered by his cloak.

"Blasphemer!" someone yelled.

Then, as some picked up stones to throw at him, he raised his head and cast his eyes to heaven.

"Father," he said aloud, that all might hear, "I thank you for having heard me. I know you always hear me—I had no need of proof. It was because of these people that I said it, that they may believe that you have sent me."

And he bared his head and cried in a loud voice, "Lazarus, come forth!"

Again there was silence. The people of Bethany, wondering how far he would dare to go, still held the stones they had picked up.

Suddenly a shadow moved in the low passage leading to

the tomb. A swathed form, bent, appeared at the foot of the steps. Susannah recognized her husband's shroud and the bag tied over his head. She sank to her knees in terror, hiding her face in her hands. Those who held stones let them fall to the ground. Two women fled. Children shrieked with fear. Martha and Mary clung to each other. The shadow leaned forward, then stopped, as if deterred by the steps.

"Help him," said the Galilean simply. "Unbind him."

Lazarus felt himself being pushed and pulled, but could see nothing. There were bandages over his eyes and in his mouth. He couldn't breathe. Someone put an arm around his waist. What was happening? He was being carried; his feet no longer touched the ground. When he was put down again, he felt a sudden wave of heat. It was as if he had been prized out of a cold, sheltered place, perhaps underground, and brought out into the sun.

He could hear voices, a distant commotion. He was being touched—on the shoulders, the stomach, the face. Why was it so dark? He tried to pull off the bag over his head, then realized he couldn't raise his arms from his sides. He called out to be untied, but could hear no sound coming from his mouth. A terrible thought struck him: perhaps he wasn't bound—perhaps he was paralyzed, dumb, blind, unable to lift even his hand.

He tried to remember. Where was he? Had he fallen ill? What was the explanation for this lassitude, this numbness in his body? And why this heat, like the sun, beating on his cold and torpid limbs? All he could remember was an abyss, in which he seemed to have been imprisoned for years.

He was being shaken. Why? He could hear voices shouting, close but indistinct. Still he couldn't breathe. At last he felt the bag being lifted from his face, and he tried to inhale. But his chest, heavy as stone, scarcely moved, and the little air he got was scorching hot. He tried to look around, to turn his head despite the stiffness in his neck. But there was a white veil before his eyes, and all he could see were patches of light, and moving shadows beyond. People were touching his mouth, his forehead, his cheeks. He was gripped from all sides, squeezed. He wanted to shout to them to let go, but could utter only a long groan.

They were untying him now, and suddenly his hands were free. But when he lifted his arm, it was as heavy as lead, and he had to let it fall again. His fear increased: these people were going to kill him, and there was nothing he could do to defend himself or escape.

He was seized by the elbows. Where were they taking him? "Let me alone, let me alone," he moaned. But no one heard or understood. His feet hit the ground. He stumbled, twisted his ankles on stones, almost fell. He had to figure out what was happening to him. But he was so tired, his whole body still so numb, the haze in his head still so thick, that he couldn't think, couldn't recall whether or not there had been an accident.

After walking for what seemed an eternity, he felt two or three men take hold of him, carry him up stairs, and lay him on a bed. Here the air was not so hot, so stifling.

At last, he thought, they'll let me rest.

But as soon as he was prone, his mouth filled with the taste of earth, and the thirst that had been constricting his throat became unbearable. He tried to swallow, but his tongue and palate, swollen and stiff, were like wood. Although he doubted that anyone could understand his moans, he begged for water. To his surprise, he felt his lips being parted and cold water being poured between his teeth—though most of it ran down his chin, neck, and shoulders. Only a trickle went into his throat, and already the cup was being taken away. He tried to sit up, to shout, but before he could, he felt gentle fingers on his cheek and hair. Opening his eyes, he saw a misty face bending over him. Soft warm lips pressed to his forehead, then everything went dark, and he sank into a deep slumber.

While Lazarus, put down by Eliphas and Joad on the bed in the upper room, was watched over by Susannah as he slept, the people of Bethany—men, women, and children—gathered outside the house. Some wanted to approach the Galilean, to throw themselves at his feet, or talk to him, touch him. But most, awed by the wonder he had just performed, hung back.

"You must be the Messiah, the one foretold by Daniel and Isaiah!" cried one of those crowding around him. "You are he who will cleanse Jerusalem of the heathen!"

"But he's a Galilean," said another. "Could the Messiah come from Galilee?"

"Is it not written," argued the water carrier, "that it is of the seed of David and out of the town of Bethlehem that the saviour of Jerusalem will be born?"

"Were you born in Bethlehem?" they asked him. "Are you the one we have been waiting for?"

"The blind see, the lame walk, the dead rise up," the

Galilean replied. "These are but signs, that men may believe in me and in the glory of my father."

"But who is your father?" asked the weaver. "Is he of the house of David?"

Before the Galilean had time to answer, there was a hubbub of voices and people were jostled aside. Two boys stood before him; they carried a woman with twisted, wasted legs.

"Heal her, Lord," they said. "She is our mother's sister and has been thus from birth. End her suffering."

The Galilean looked at the cripple without a word, then turned and went into the house. As the two boys started to follow, the big man with the goatee roughly barred their way.

By the eighth hour, the yard outside the house swarmed with people. Dozens from Jerusalem waited there. Many were barefoot, with cloaks and tunics in tatters, and they leaned on crutches, or had grimy bandages around their heads or over their eyes. Blind men groped, their sticks held out in front of them; paralytics, carried on planks, had themselves laid down as near as possible to the resurrected carpenter's door. Even a leper crept up, trembling. But as soon as the others saw his tainted body and the terrible cracked and corroded mask with which the disease had covered his face, they drove him off, crying, "Unclean! Unclean!" and the wretch had to flee to avoid being stoned.

The Galilean, shut up in the house, would not come out. Martha and Mary stayed with him. Sitting on the floor with his back against the wall, he conversed with the big man and his friends: a blond youth called John, who had been with him the time he came here to hide, and another, with thick curly hair, whose name was Judas. The Galilean took no notice of the noise outside, the loud cries imploring him to perform more miracles.

Susannah meanwhile had not stirred from the upper room. She would not leave Lazarus even for a second. She knelt by the bed, her eyes full of tears, gazing at him and wondering, unable to believe in his resurrection.

Was he breathing? His terribly hollow chest scarcely moved. But yes, she heard him—a hoarse sound, like that before he died. What if he were to die again! But the Galilean said he was out of danger, and it was impossible now to doubt the Galilean.

Then why couldn't she rejoice?

Because that gray face frightened her. The bloodless, colorless lips, the dark rings around the eyes, the gaunt, bony body. His features were familiar but unfamiliar, twisted in an expression of suffering and terror.

She would wake up and find she had been dreaming. No one had really rolled away the heavy boulder that closed the entrance to the tomb. Lazarus still lay there stiffly in the dark, in his shroud, face covered, arms bound, hands and feet swathed in bandages. . . . And yet certain details seemed real enough. The strange odor of damp earth that clung to Lazarus's body. The smell of mud mixed with aloes and rancid oils—how could she be dreaming that?

Lazarus was alive, lying there before her very eyes. Yet that pale, shrunken face was not his. That ashen hair and beard did not belong to him.

She didn't know what to think.

She told herself that, returned so recently from the region of darkness, he could not yet be as he had been before. In a few days, his new life would restore his strength and beauty. But she couldn't convince herself.

Overcoming the slight repugnance she felt toward this strange body, she finally made herself bend over it. She told herself that Lazarus, her husband, really was there asleep in front of her, miraculously alive. Then she forgot her fear and, with a quickly beating heart, covered his brow, lips, and neck with loving kisses.

In the evening Martha served supper to the Galilean and his three companions, fritters of flour and honey. Mary approached the table bearing a jar of costly perfume—the spikenard from distant India that Susannah had used to anoint Lazarus's body five days earlier—and poured some on the Galilean's head. Seeing that he made no objection, she knelt before him, removed his sandals, and emptied the rest over his ankles and feet, which were white with the dust from the road. The whole house filled with the penetrating scent. But Peter, the big man, and the other whose name was Judas were shocked and said, "What extravagance! This perfume could have been sold for much money. We haven't taken in a single coin for four days. We're down to our last two."

Mary paused and looked up at the Galilean, afraid of having displeased him.

"Let her alone," he said. "She is doing me a kindness. She was keeping the perfume against the day of my burial. You worry too much about the money people give or do not give when you hold out your hand, or the money that you have or do not have in your belt. I say to you that Mary will be remembered throughout the world for what she has just done."

"Do you mean to stay here for some days?" asked Judas after a long silence.

"No," replied the Galilean. "We shall leave as soon as we've finished our meal."

"So we're going back at last to Jerusalem!"

"The hour is not yet come. We must go first to Ephraim."

"But that takes us into the wilderness!" said Peter. "Who will feed us there?"

"Have I not provided for you myself, when we were without food on the bare hills? What I did this morning isn't enough for you. Consider this woman—she scarcely knows me and yet she believes in me. You have followed me for two years and still you doubt. Woe to him who cannot see what is before his eyes!"

When he finished speaking, Mary, knowing that his anger was not directed at her, dried his feet with her long hair and kissed them.

Later in the evening, when it was dark, the Galilean put on the cloak made of two blankets sewn together, and the three women prostrated themselves again before him.

"We shall never forget what you have done," said Mary. "We shall bear witness to it until our last breath."

He smiled, told them to rise, and opened the door to go.

Despite the biting cold, there were still many cripples and beggars outside, gathered around big fires. As soon as they saw the Galilean, those who had the use of their legs hurried over to him.

"Heal us, Lord!," they cried. "We believe in you! You are the Messiah! Heal us!"

The big man pushed them aside, and the Galilean, with Judas and a young man with fair hair, made his way past them through the courtyard. He had to shake off a few who clung to his cloak asking for pity. Martha, watching him go, could see by the light of the flames the shiny pointed helmets of a couple of Temple guards, and the white tunic and conical hat of a priest. So, she thought, the people in Jerusalem—the Sadducees and the priest—know about the miracle he performed this morning. She was suddenly afraid. Wouldn't they regard this as yet another reason to fear him, hate him, even kill him?

She gazed after the man she now believed to be the true saviour of his people, until he vanished in the darkness, in the direction of the hills and the wilderness. Then she closed the door and went in to Susannah, to her sister, Mary, and to her brother, Lazarus, risen from the dead.

Susannah stayed beside Lazarus all night.

At the first hour, at dawn, thinking he would soon wake up, see her, and speak to her, she decided to pretty herself for him, so he would recognize her and love her again.

She took her mirror of polished metal and her ivory comb into the other room. There, out of sight, she braided her hair and decorated it with colored ribbons. When she was satisfied with her coiffure, she attended to her eyes. Dipping a spatula into one of the pots of cosmetics, she waited until her hand stopped trembling before carefully applying the blue-black lead compound to her eyelids and brows. After that, she reddened her lips and cheeks with powdered *sikra*, and rubbed her hands with the dark-yellow ashes obtained from alkanna leaves.

With brows and lashes darkened, cheeks flushed, and eyelids and palms tinted, she looked thoughtfully at her reflection. Had she put on too much? No, that was how Lazarus
liked it. She continued with the ritual of her toilet.

On went her round earrings, gold as the sun, and her best
dress of fine linen trimmed with ribbons of silk and wool.
Then, of the two jars of perfume standing beside the mirror,
she took the cylindrical one, sniffed it, then decided on the
bulbous one, which contained myrrh. She put a drop of the
essence behind each ear, on her cheeks, and finally on her
lips.

Draping a shawl over her shoulders, she fastened it with
a silver buckle set with pearls and precious stones.

Now, satisfied that she would look attractive to her husband, she put away comb, mirror, spatula, pots, and jars,
and returned to the upper room.

She waited all morning for Lazarus to wake.

Toward noon, he stirred and uttered a few incomprehensible words. But, alas, his face remained gray and his body
cold; the smell of damp that hung about him was as strong
as ever. The air seemed to stick in his throat, as if he were
about to stop breathing. But after a few seconds, his chest
would begin rising and falling again. Susannah was worried.
She was sorry she had let the Galilean go without telling him
how ill her husband seemed.

At last, near the eighth hour, Lazarus opened his eyes.

The first thing he saw was Susannah's face. Although it
appeared to him only through a mist, he recognized her wide
full mouth, which seemed strangely red. He recognized, too,
her braided hair flecked with patches of color, as if decked
with ribbons for some festivity. He stretched out his hand

toward her, and tried to sit up, but he hadn't the strength, and fell back again on the bed.

"Susannah . . ." he murmured.

She came very close. He noticed a long shiny streak running down her cheek. Why was she crying? Then he remembered the bag that had been over his face, and how his arms and legs had been tied. He remembered his thirst, the sweltering, stifling heat, and the people touching him, moving him. . . .

"Am I ill?" he asked. "Where are the people who were shouting and trying to hurt me?"

He could scarcely hear himself speak; the words from his mouth were almost indistinguishable.

"No one was trying to hurt you," she answered. "The Galilean revived you—brought you out of the Great Sleep. You were dead for five days, and he brought you back to life."

What, he thought, have we arrived at the day of the last judgment?

"No man, Susannah, has the power to do that," he said.

And yet the taste of earth in his mouth, the icy chill that numbed his body, the memory deep inside him of the bottomless pit—these spoke of death.

He asked to get up. Helped by his two sisters, he went to the big room downstairs that served as kitchen and dining room. Unable to move around unaided, he reclined, rather than sat, on a divan, the kind used for guests on special occasions. He looked about him: was he really in his own house? Although he could see things only through a curtain of mist, which made them blurred and almost colorless, he recognized the whitewashed walls, the two narrow windows that were the only openings, the mud floor, the broad beams supporting the ceiling, the wood- and peat-burning stove, the low door, the stools, the bags, jars, and boxes, the table, the chairs padded with cloth or straw.

"Would you like something to eat?" asked Martha. "I just baked some bread. You've been back with us more than a day and haven't eaten a thing."

He thought for a moment: was he hungry? No, not really—though he still suffered from thirst. But water did not remove the taste of mud that kept coming into his mouth.

"A cup of wine," he said, making an effort to pronounce every word as clearly as possible. It was so hard to utter the least sound. "I'd like some wine."

"Wouldn't you rather have a piece of bread and some dried fish?" asked Martha.

He shook his head: no, just wine.

But when he drank from the cup his sister held to his lips, an unbearable burning sensation spread inside him. At the second sip he knew he would not be able to keep the wine down. He tried to hold it at the bottom of his throat, but it flooded back into his mouth, and he spat it out. Susannah rushed to him, but he put out his arm, warding her off, and painfully raised his hand to his face to wipe his beard and chin.

A shout reached him from outside, a cry full of angry challenge.

"Lazarus! The man brought back to life! Show yourself—we want to see you!"

Outside, too, in the courtyard of his own house, they were calling him "the man brought back to life"!

He asked to be helped up and taken to the window—to him, just a bright patch in the vagueness of the wall. At first, the brilliant daylight so dazzled his eyes, he couldn't keep them open. Other voices were raised on all sides.

"There he is! There he is!"

"Come out and tell us about it!"

"Did you see Abraham?"

"Did you see David?"

The voices swelled into a dull roar.

"They've been waiting and calling out for you since yesterday," said Martha gently. "You ought to go to the door and let them see you."

Slowly, Lazarus forced his eyes open. Despite the blinding, burning white light he could see a large number of people gathered outside his house.

What did they want? Had the Galilean, whom he could hardly remember, really brought him back to life? True, Isaiah had said: "Dead men shall live. . . . Awake and sing, ye that dwell in dust: for the earth shall cast out the dead." But Isaiah was talking about the day of the last judgment and eternal life. And that day, that time of reward and punishment, had not yet come.

He couldn't breathe, a wave of vertigo made the courtyard teeter. He clutched at the wall to keep from falling. His hand encountered Susannah's dress. The three women helped him back to bed.

"It's a dream," he muttered. "Soon I'll wake up and everything will be as it was before."

As he approached Bethany, Haggai, a priest and influential member of the Sanhedrin, saw that he had not been lied to. Just as Zerah and several other witnesses had said, there was still a crowd on the outskirts of the village nearly a week after the "miracle." There were even a few tents pitched on the hill, and now, at noon, many of the people were cooking fish over wood fires. They were not likely to move on in a hurry. Some poor folk sat or lay waiting by the side of the road, in the sun, staring into space. About thirty women were jostling one another at the well, trying to lower their pitchers into the water. Children rushed in all directions, chasing, fighting, rolling about in the dust. Newcomers on their donkeys shouted for others to make way.

Suddenly Haggai heard wild yells behind him, and turned to see four men restraining a fifth, a madman who slavered at the mouth and writhed like one possessed. How long would the Romans tolerate such disorder?

The nearer he came to the village, the denser grew the crowd. He stepped over the inert body of a drunk collapsed across his path. A beggar caught at his cloak and held out his hand, saying, "A coin, give me a coin, and the Almighty will requite you." He had to give him a kick to get rid of him.

Haggai was astonished to find such an assemblage of ragamuffins and cripples in the courtyard outside Lazarus's house. He passed a little girl lying on a plank. Her face was covered with yellow scabs, suppurating sores, and the buzzing cloud of flies that these attracted. All the destitute of Jerusalem seemed to have gathered here. One of them, leaning on crutches padded with rags, accosted the priest.

"Do you know where the Messiah is?" he asked. "They say he's back at Lazarus's. Is that true?"

Haggai, pushing his way through the repulsive crowd, did not answer.

24

He had to bang on the door half a dozen times, shouting who he was, before it opened. When he entered, the door was shut behind him at once, the latch lowered, and the key turned.

The three women who greeted him did so without warmth. He sensed at once that they were afraid of him, mistrustful. It did not surprise him. Everyone knew that the Sanhedrin, the priests, the scribes, and the Sadducees all hated the "Messiah" from Galilee.

Without waiting to be asked, Haggai sat down on a stool and asked to see Lazarus, son of Chaim.

"He's sleeping," said one of the women. "We must let him rest."

"Wake him," said Haggai. "He has nothing to fear from me—I don't come here as an enemy. All I want is to ask him a few questions. About Jesus of Galilee. You may not know it, but that man has already performed thirty-four miracles, and now all Judea is in an uproar. I myself met a blind man named Jair who had his sight restored by him at the Pool of Siloam. If Jesus can bring the dead back to life as well, we ought to know about it."

The three women withdrew and briefly consulted. To refuse the priest's request, they decided, would only arouse his suspicions, so they went to wake Lazarus, asleep in the upper room.

Meanwhile, a growing crowd of hotheads outside demanded to be allowed to see the Messiah and Lazarus, the man brought back from the dead. Their yelling, and the unrest it implied, alarmed the priest.

This is reason enough for Jesus to be got rid of, he thought.

When Lazarus appeared, leaning on Martha, the tallest

and strongest of the three women, Haggai felt a gust of cold air in the room, though the windows were closed. Having been present when physicians interviewed some of the people on whom miracles had been performed, Haggai did not doubt the Galilean's power. But not for a moment did he believe this story of a resurrection. The man now approaching him slowly, however, really looked like one risen from the grave.

Lazarus dropped onto the divan and half lay on a heap of cushions. His young wife sat beside him. Haggai noticed her swollen eyelids; she had clearly been crying.

Lazarus had difficulty breathing: the air came from his chest fitfully, whistling. Haggai stared at him and grew more and more uneasy. The dull gray of the man's face, a face so thin that the bones stuck out, irresistibly suggested a death mask. Haggai had seen the same expression on many corpses— an expression of pain or fear that made the features look drawn and traced a deep furrow in the brow. Although he was some distance away, he could smell the odor that came from Lazarus's body, a vague mixture of damp earth and rancid oils. When Lazarus turned his eyes toward him, he saw at once that they were strangely dim. The priest looked away, his pride and self-assurance gone.

He hated the thought of death.

He had come here confident that he could collect enough proof to denounce this scandalous fraud and expose and destroy the Galilean at last. Instead, he was struck dumb in the presence of an incomprehensible man with colorless lips, a hollow chest, and hair and beard as dull as ashes.

For a moment he regretted that he had come. But the reason he was there was important enough to overcome this disquiet.

26

He pulled himself together, then looked Lazarus in the face again.

"We have heard a rumor in Jerusalem," he said, speaking slowly. "They say Jesus, son of Joseph, brought you back to life. Some say they saw you leave the tomb five days after your death. Is it true?"

He paused. The dim eyes looked at him. The silence was broken only by the shouting outside and the man's labored breathing.

"You must tell me whether this man really did wake you from the Great Sleep," said Haggai louder.

Lazarus appeared to hesitate. He looked at the three women standing near him, then bowed his head, as if afraid to tell the truth.

"You have nothing to fear from me," the priest went on. "But you must realize that if such a marvel has taken place, the Sanhedrin has to know about it."

For a long while Lazarus said nothing. Haggai, watching him, thought, The man is a ghost. Can that "miracle worker" have really raised the dead? And if so, who is he and what does he want? What is his purpose?

And how could he, one of the Galilean's fiercest opponents, explain to the high priest and the assembled judges that they would have to abandon hope of dismissing the Bethany affair as a fraud? No—he was letting shock get the better of him and jumping to conclusions.

Yet how could he explain this face, these eyes, the smell? How could he account for the darkness that filled the room despite the lighted brazier? And even if the Galilean *could* bring the dead back to life, that did not prove he was the

Messiah. Elijah had possessed the same power, and he had been only a prophet, not the saviour of Israel.

At last Lazarus spoke. Haggai felt a chill sweep over him.

"I don't know," said Lazarus, speaking with great effort. "But everyone tells me I was dead and that the Galilean revived me."

His voice was faint and seemed to come from his chest. He did not articulate, hardly moved his mouth. Each word was broken into parts, and the jerky sounds were barely comprehensible. His young wife sat beside him, her head bowed, as though not daring to look at him.

"I can remember being at the bottom of a black pit," Lazarus went on. "They tell me that when he said 'Arise,' I got up and walked. . . . All I remember then is the bag over my head, the bonds tying my arms to my body, people shouting and pushing me, and the awful heat."

He stopped to draw breath. The stamp of suffering on his face grew deeper.

"You saw nothing in the black pit?" asked Haggai.

"Nothing," the low voice answered.

"Not Abraham? Not David? Try to remember."

"I saw nothing but the black pit . . . only the black pit."

If the man had wanted to deceive him, Haggai thought, he would at least have invented something. He would have mentioned the mysterious place referred to in the Scriptures as *sheol*, the region of darkness where the dead wandered. Many people believed that one could enter that realm of silence by moving aside the boulder in the middle of the Holy of Holies, which guarded the entrance. No, unfortunately, this man was not lying. No one could feign such suffering and such fear.

28

The problem was more complex, more serious. Although anxious to leave, to get away from Lazarus as soon as possible, Haggai turned to the women.

"And you," he asked, "do you agree that the Galilean brought Lazarus back to life?"

"Yes," answered Martha. "We were present at the miracle and promised to bear witness to it."

"In that case, tell me everything that happened."

Martha obeyed, though with visible reluctance as she related the facts, from her brother's death to his emerging from the tomb. Haggai, who had heard what had taken place from several witnesses, listened carefully. Noticing that Martha did not quote the Galilean's exact words, the priest concluded that she was trying to shield him. He already knew that the Galilean had blasphemed atrociously by saying that people should believe in him, when one should believe in nothing but the Almighty.

As Martha spoke, the rabble outside grew increasingly impatient. Some now banged on the door.

"Is it because I'm here?" Haggai asked.

"No," said Mary. "It's been like this for five days. They want to see Lazarus and the Galilean."

As soon as Martha finished her story, the priest rose. He knew everything now, except the answer to one question.

"Where is this Jesus now?" he asked.

"We don't know," lied Martha.

What does it matter? thought Haggai as he left. He is bound to perform more miracles. He wants people to believe in him too much to stay hidden for long.

On his way back to Jerusalem, Haggai felt as if he, too,

had emerged from a tomb and was coming back to life as he breathed the keen air. But he was so shaken by the encounter that he had still not put his thoughts in order by the time he reached the city.

Back home in the wealthy district of the Hasmonaean Palace, he noticed the smell of damp earth and rancid oil in his clothes. He hastily undressed and washed his hands and face.

It was ten days now since Lazarus left his tomb.

People were saying that the Galilean was back in Jerusalem. The report of his triumphal entry into the city was enough to empty the streets of Bethany. Sufferers and sightseers departed in search of the Messiah, until no one remained in the courtyard outside the house.

Lazarus slept less now, and his mind was clearing. But he was still unable to walk unaided, and still did not eat or go out. His face was ashen; the smell clung to his body. Everything seemed empty to him, deserted, both within and without. Susannah, watching him carefully, every movement, every reaction, saw no improvement. He was gloomier and more ailing every day. She began to fear that the happiness she had once known would never return.

Perhaps she, too, should go to Jerusalem to find the Galilean. If she told him how ill Lazarus was, he might return with her to Bethany and perform a second miracle, to make Lazarus as he used to be. He could not have brought him back to life simply to let him live as he was now. But the Galilean had refused, once before, to come and heal Lazarus, so there was no way to know if he would come again. She hesitated. Perhaps it was too soon. Perhaps Lazarus should

30

be given time to get his strength back. Also, much as she loved Lazarus, she dreaded the thought of setting out for Jerusalem alone.

One morning, Lazarus felt better. For the first time, he managed to get up by himself; he put on his tunic and fastened his sandals without the help of Martha or Susannah. He even succeeded in getting down the stairs, by leaning his back against the wall and descending carefully, one step at a time. When he reached the main room, he went slowly to the divan and sat down to get his breath back. His breathing was still hoarse and shallow, but the weight that had been on his chest seemed lighter now.

Hope sprang up within him.

As soon as Susannah got back from filling her pitcher at the well, he told her what he had done unaided. His voice was stronger. "Perhaps, in time," he said to his young wife, "I'll be as I was before."

At noon, though he was not hungry, he made himself eat a little dried herring and drank a whole cup of water. But the taste of earth still in his mouth was stronger than the taste of the food, even the pungent flavor of the fish. That did not matter, though: the main thing was to swallow something without vomiting it up again.

After the meal, he said he wanted to go up to the roof. He climbed the stairs with the help of a crutch made in his own workshop some years ago. On the roof, the blinding light forced him to shut his eyes. He felt dizzy and moved away from the edge. From the heat of the sun and the warm breeze, he knew it was spring. Wanting to see the flowers that had burst from the earth, he slowly forced himself to open his eyes and to keep them open despite the glare.

The village street, the vineyards, the fields planted with olive and fig trees were all there, but he could not see the wide garish-blue sweep of the sky, the tawny red of the earth and the distant hills, the mauve, lavender-blue, and gold masses of crocuses contrasting with the pink of the almond trees. He saw only dull shapes, grays. This was not the landscape he used to love. Although noon was not long past, it seemed early evening. As he gazed at the pallid wilderness, his heart sank, and the flicker of hope of that morning vanished.

Was this the world he would have to live in now?

At the tenth hour, he went into his workshop. Disheartened from his experience on the roof, he was troubled by the thought that he might not be able to work again. He must work with wood, without a moment's delay. If he waited too long, everyone in the village would think he was lazy, useless. That, he could not endure.

In his shop, which had been shut since his death, he felt a pang on seeing the pine and cedar beams stacked against the wall, just as he had left them, and the trunks of hard sycamore to be made into plowshares. Leaning on his crutch, he went over to the bench. He could feel the familiar shavings and sawdust under his feet. He examined his tools: ax, hammers, plane, adz, knives, square, clamp—everything exactly as on the evening before he fell ill. He looked at the chest he had started making for Saul, and the doorposts and lintels he had almost finished for Daniel's new house.

A lump rose in his throat. Would he ever be able to finish them? What am I, he thought, without the trade I love and live by? He turned to the plank lying on the bench, and took down his best saw. Propping himself up on his crutch, he started to work. Twice he drew the saw across the wood, but the blade made no impression. He applied more force, but felt only how weak his shoulder, how limp his fingers were. His wrist gave way, and the saw slipped out of his hand. He collapsed onto a stool.

"I'm no good for anything anymore," he muttered. "Who will earn the money to feed and clothe us? And how can I live without fulfilling the commandment Jehovah gave to the first man—to earn his bread by the sweat of his brow?"

He saw himself in rags, begging at the side of the road like the poor wretches who had filled his courtyard a few days ago. He *must* get his strength back. He must pray for it, and force himself to eat, to go out to take walks. He would come to the shop every morning, until he could saw the plank.

At the door, he was again blinded by the sun. But he waited for his eyes to adjust to the light. Then he walked for a dozen or so paces in the courtyard. But when he turned to the house, it looked as though a layer of ashes had fallen on it, making it dirty, dilapidated, ugly.

It was Sabbath eve. Martha, back from buying fish, dates, and figs for the next day's meals, supervised the baking; Mary filled the Sabbath lamp with oil.

Shortly before it was time for the evening meal, Susannah, who was finishing a thorough cleaning of the house, saw her husband come out of the workshop, as he did every evening. She noticed he had fastened his leather carpenter's belt around his waist, just as he used to do when he cut wood. He looked exhausted, his face more serious and sorrowful than on previous evenings, and he was using his crutch again. Anxious as she was, she let him go past her and up the stairs, one by one, without asking him what he had done at his bench in the shop.

In the upper room, Lazarus undressed. Again he looked at his pitiable body. He had been trying to saw that plank for five days. But the blade would not bite into the wood, and he kept dropping the saw. He touched his weak, wasted arm, his bony elbow; he loathed the feel of his dry skin. His hand traveled up to his shoulder. . . . No, it was no use—the muscles were as flabby as ever! Would he ever work again? This evening, his legs could scarcely carry him, as if no longer able to bear the weight of his body, slight as it was. He touched the cut on his hand from the saw. Although the wound was deep, it had not bled, and, strangely, he had felt no pain. In fact, apart from the burning sensation in his chest the time he tried to drink some wine after he rose from the grave, there had been no pain at all. Only an occasional faint twinge in his back or neck.

He could not stand the sight of his jutting ribs and hollow, wrinkled belly. He must wash himself again, try once more to scrub that grayness from his skin. Using the natron from Egypt, with which he used to cleanse himself of all impurity before the Sabbath, he soaped himself from head to foot, then rubbed himself as hard as he could, until night began to fall and the hazzan sounded the ram's horn three times from the roof of the tallest house in the village to tell everyone to light their lamps and let the Sabbath shine.

At the first hour next day, Susannah was surprised to see Lazarus come down from the upper room in his trimmed and

34

embroidered ceremonial tunic, with a broad silk sash wound several times around his waist. The garment looked ridiculously large on his wasted body. The neck was loose and showed the top of his hollow chest; the sleeves, though turned up, were too long and too wide; the hyacinth-blue ritual tassels dangled almost to his feet. From his body, masking the odor of his skin, came the scent of rosemary and marjoram.

"I'm not going to the synagogue this morning," he said, "but I've rubbed myself with sweet-smelling herbs, eaten some perfumed pepper, and dressed in honor of the Almighty."

The sun had just risen, so they sat down to eat and observe the Sabbath ritual.

Lazarus insisted on reciting the threefold blessing himself. Then he was the first to break the bread Martha had made. Susannah watched him eat a few dates and dried figs and drink almost a whole cup of scented wine without spitting out a drop. He was better, she thought.

He was eating again: not much, but regularly. Twice a day he would have some fruit, and five or six mouthfuls of bread or fish. He walked about the house alone, merely putting a hand against the wall. Every afternoon he walked around the courtyard a few times with the aid of his crutch. He seemed to breathe more easily; he spoke more clearly; and, most important, he shut himself up every day in his shop, no doubt to get back into the habit of working. True, he always came out dejected, and with sorrow in his face.

He still frightened her. His breath was still cold, his body gaunt and thin, his back bent, as if carrying an invisible burden, and the smell of death still clung to his skin. But Susannah tried to persuade herself that eventually he would

35

be the same as before. He spoke more and more often of getting his strength back, and that must surely be because he felt it gradually returning.

Lazarus noticed Susannah watching him. He smiled at her and reminded himself yet again that here was something beautiful and very dear before his eyes. But on her, too, despite the ribbons and the reddened lips, a layer of ashes seemed to have fallen. He looked at his sisters, Martha and Mary, who had divided a wheaten cake between them, and he felt like a stranger in their midst, an intruder in their lives.

Early as it was, he heard children playing merrily in the street outside. He thought how he, too, had once been happy to be alive. And, for the first time, he thought the Galilean would have done better to leave him in his tomb.

When the meal was over, he wanted to pray. He asked Susannah to tie the phylacteries to his brow. She laid his white silk tallith over his head and shoulders, then helped him kneel in the direction of Jerusalem and the Temple, standing by to support him.

First he recited the Shema softly. "Hear, O Israel: The Lord our God, the Lord is One. And thou shalt love the Lord thy God with all thy heart, with all thy soul, and with all thy might. . . ." Then he lifted up his hands and continued, louder, with the eighteen blessings, praising and glorifying the God of Abraham, Isaac, and Jacob, "great, mighty and terrible, giver of all blessings."

With head bowed and eyes closed, he asked forgiveness for his sins and begged the Almighty to give him his daily bread.

Finally, he prostrated himself full length on the floor, so

Susannah had to let go of him. She tried to lift him but he pushed her away. With his forehead pressed to the ground, he implored the Lord to give him back his strength.

The following day, Lazarus asked Susannah to go up the hill with him.

"I want to walk with no one's help but yours," he said. "I need to get out of the house. To go farther than the courtyard."

Waiting until his eyes could withstand the glare of the sun, until through the usual curtain of gray he could make out the straight dusty street bordered by square whitewashed houses like his own, he took Susannah's arm, and they set out.

He walked with a limp, and his ankles gave whenever he stepped on a stone. The people of Bethany, seeing him for the first time since his miraculous resurrection, stopped what they were doing and stood at their doors to watch him pass. But they were silent, surprised by his uncertain gait, ashen face, and shrunken body. When they recalled his former strength and beauty, it seemed to them that the Galilean, despite his power, had not been able to drive death away completely. Many were so upset by the sight that they stayed indoors until Lazarus left the village.

So that's why he hasn't shown himself, they thought.

Lazarus and Susannah, clinging together, climbed the hill. They had to stop every twenty paces for Lazarus to catch his breath.

"That doesn't matter," he said. "I'm walking better today. I'll get to the top of the hill. And tomorrow I'll go farther. Soon, I'll set out, by myself, on the road to Jerusalem, to pray in the Temple."

But his feet stumbled on the stones more and more, and he had to hold Susannah's arm more tightly to keep from falling. The wheezing and the panting became as bad as they had been on the evening after his resurrection. When they reached the top of the hill, he lay down exhausted. Susannah lay beside him.

"You are right," she whispered in his ear. "You are much better. Your strength is returning. Soon you'll be able to go to the Temple."

She stroked his cheek, happy that his efforts had been rewarded. When she pushed the hair from his forehead, the skin was warm, not cold, as it had been. His face now seemed less pale, less dry and wrinkled. The smell seemed to have gone, too, and she wondered whether his beard was not growing blacker every day, and his lips redder.

Forgetting her fear, she brushed his brow with her lips. When he opened his eyes, she took him in her arms. They stayed like that for some time.

After his breathing became quieter, more regular, he put his arms around her and gently kissed her neck. She touched his belly, hips, thighs, forgetting the shriveled skin beneath her fingers. Slipping her hand between his legs, she began to caress him.

He held her close as her little white hand moved between his thighs. Loosening her shawl, undoing the fastenings of her tunic, he put his hand on her burning breast. Their faces touched; he could feel the throb of her blood under the fine, soft skin and could see the whiteness of her teeth. Why shouldn't she impart to him some of her youth and life?

Her warmth spread over him. She turned her head slightly, and her long curly hair fell over his face and into his mouth.

Why could he no longer smell its scent? He bit the golden crescent of her earring, then moved his head down toward her bare shoulder. Through the veil of ashes it was difficult to make out the varying shades of her skin. The region of her face seemed bright above her dazzling white neck. Her bosom was darker, like honey.

Susannah's breathing grew rapid and shallow. She sat up on his belly, still caressing him, but no excitement or pleasure rose in him. She shook her head, then tossed it back, eyes closed, lips parted. Should he not ask her to stop, to put an end to this useless business? She rested the palm of her free hand on him. How could she bear to touch his clammy body? He touched her fingers, started to take them toward his mouth, to bite them, but the thought of his dry tongue made him desist. Instead, he stroked her rounded hips. She moved her head back and forth, her neck arching smoothly.

"I love you, Susannah," he whispered.

Again she lay on him, her hands moving more and more desperately. Again he felt the throbbing within the breast pressed to his—a throbbing so strong, he could hear it. Alas, in him there was no such pulse of desire.

She continued trying to arouse the limp gray wrinkled thing that probably never again would visit her straight and full and strong. A surge of tears pressed at his throat, but he could no longer weep.

"Stop," he said. "It's no use."

They set off for home. He still clung to her, leaning on her arm. They went down the hill without a word. As soon as they reached the house, Lazarus, in exhaustion and despair, lay down alone in the upper room.

After a while, Susannah followed.

"Do not worry," she said. "Your desire will come back as strong as ever, and next spring I shall give you the son you want so much."

He smiled at her. How he loved her for her kindness, her youth, the sweetness of her ways. But despite her effort to conceal her sadness and anxiety, he could read them in her face, in her eyes. What would happen if he could no longer satisfy her? In accordance with rabbinic teaching, the assembled judges would make him divorce her, and she would go back to live with her father at the other end of the village.

In the middle of the night, unable to sleep, he moved close to Susannah and put his leg against hers, pressed his belly against her hip, moved until they were breast to breast. She stirred, rolled her head toward him, and he could feel her breath on his cheek. Carefully he touched her face, and in the darkness of the room felt, below her closed eyelids, two small tears drying on her cheeks.

Lazarus, who had spent whole days sleeping when he first returned from the grave, now could not sleep at all. He tossed and turned from the first hour of the night until the last. He threw away his pillows and tried lying flat, then retrieved them and put them under his neck. Suddenly cold, he wrapped himself in the blanket; then just as suddenly he was hot and threw it off again. Although he often moved close to Susannah, as she lay beside him, he would move away again almost at once, for fear of offending her, repelling her by his smell or by the coldness of his skin. Whatever he did, whatever position he tried, he stayed awake, and was preyed upon by melancholy thoughts.

He wondered whether the Galilean had not exhausted his power when he brought him out of the tomb. Perhaps all the man could do was return a corpse to the state it was in before the moment of death. There was a difference between raising a dead man and restoring him to life, to all life's happiness and warmth. Lazarus was terrified by this thought—for if all the Galilean could do was merely awaken the dead, then he, Lazarus, had not the slightest chance of truly living again.

One night, unable to bear lying awake, he rose, wrapped himself in his cloak, and went up to the roof. There, looking out into the darkness, he recalled how he used to love these cold nights before Passover. He had breathed in the smells of warm earth and wild plants; had listened to the thousands of faint sounds quickening the enormous silence; had gazed at the multitude of stars dotting the blue-black sky and shedding a mist of light over the hills. Now, he could not smell the spring or hear its rustlings. He could not see the constellation of Orion, which he knew was twinkling on the horizon beyond Jericho and the dark wall of Jebel Qarantal.

Imprisoned in an impenetrable fog, all he could do was shiver from the cold.

What had happened to him made no sense: no one came back again after death! Perhaps he was dreaming, and all these dull, distorted images and sounds were merely passing before him during his Great Sleep. Perhaps it was a punishment for his sins. But what sins did he commit that were wicked enough for the Almighty to afflict and abandon him like this?

There were, he thought, signs that actually he was still dead. The fact that he never felt hunger or thirst. Though he made himself drink and eat a little bread or fruit, he did so not out of inclination or need, but in the hope of regaining some of his strength. The fact that he could no longer make love to his wife. And this astonishing ability to do entirely without sleep.

He had a sudden urge to throw himself off the roof and put an end to this nightmare. His feet were near the edge. If he leaned forward, he would lose his balance and fall. But he hesitated. What other terrible punishment awaited him if he deliberately destroyed himself? Or, instead of falling to his death, might he not just injure himself, break both legs or his back on the stones of the courtyard and be unable ever to walk again—and this time permanently? The house was not that high. . . .

He stepped back and tried to remember the bottomless pit in which he had been imprisoned for so long. But all he could recall was a hole without walls, a kind of well, in the middle of which he had been suspended. So there was nothing after death: the body simply returned to clay, and the soul, instead of being borne aloft by an angel, sank slowly into an infinite abyss.

He went back to bed and lay down again beside the sleeping Susannah.

Soon, he thought, I'll be able to go to Jerusalem alone, and I'll seek out the Galilean and at least get him to tell me whether I'm alive or dead.

Next day at sunrise, he counted the money left in the house—his earnings from the days when he still worked. He put aside the coins needed for the next payment of taxes to the Romans and calculated what remained for daily expenses. All that was left for the women to use at the market were four shekels of silver and sixteen shekels in small copper coins. Soon, how

42

would they be able to live? Never, despite his infirmities, would he lower himself so far as to beg in the streets of Bethany or Jerusalem. "He who does not work has no right to eat," said the Scriptures. He must, without fail, go back to his job again as soon as possible. Or someone else would take his place: Bethany could not do without a carpenter for long. Eliphas, his apprentice, begged almost every day to be allowed to use his master's tools to finish the chest ordered by Saul and the lintels for which Daniel was still waiting.

Not wasting another moment, he shut himself in his workshop, took hold of the saw with both hands, braced his thighs against the bench, and fit the serrated edge into the notch he had managed to make in the plank after days of effort. Shutting his eyes, he concentrated as hard as he could. He thought of Eliphas using his tools, of Eliphas being looked up to and respected in the village as he had once been. He saw himself shrunken, in rags, holding out his hand for alms as he lay on the steps by the Pool of Siloam. With that, he summoned his remaining strength into his shoulders, arms, and wrists, and pressed frantically down and forward on the saw. It slipped out of the notch. He drew it back, to try again, but it fell from his grasp to the floor.

He did not pick it up. He went back to the upper room and sat on the bed. It's no use trying, he thought. I'll never be able to use a tool again. I'm a corpse, reanimated but without the breath of life.

After the evening meal, he told Susannah: "Tomorrow I go to Jerusalem. I will find the Galilean and show him the state that I am in, and ask him to tell me what his powers are. If he really can raise the dead, I will ask him to perform another and even greater miracle."

Next day, as the sun was rising, Lazarus left the house. Susannah wanted to go with him, but he insisted on going alone.

"Don't worry if I'm not back this evening," he told her. "I will not come home until I've spoken with the Galilean."

He took his cloak and a stout staff, kissed his wife and sisters good-bye, and set out, limping, on the road to Jerusalem.

When he reached the Mount of Olives, he found himself in the midst of a crowd of pilgrims from Jericho or Betharaba, come to celebrate Passover. Tired and breathless, he sat down on a large flat stone. The surrounding hills were covered with tents. He recognized people from Jaffa and Caesarea, west of the city, who had come through Gareb; others from Galilee, who had had a shorter journey; and still others from Samaria, Capernaum, Nain, and Ephrem, all white with dust as they came in hundreds down the slopes of Mount Scopus. Worn out from their long journey on foot or on donkeys, they prostrated themselves at the sight of the holy city, some of them moved to tears. He could hear them singing: "I was glad when they said unto me, let us go into the house of the Lord."

He remembered how he had come for Passover last year with Susannah, Martha, and Mary. He remembered buying the lamb without spot or blemish required by the Law, and giving it, for sacrifice, to the priests at the entrance to their courtyard. He saw in his mind's eye the return to Bethany and the meal in the upper room. They had recited the psalms about the exodus from Egypt; they had shared the unleavened bread and the first cup of wine, and eaten pieces of the sacrificial lamb, roasted and served with bitter herbs. Later, dressed in their best, they had sung in the streets and joined Joad and Eliphas in a rhythmic dance around the houses. When night fell, the whole village had formed a great circle in the torchlight. He had held Susannah's hand. He could still hear her laughter—bright, joyous, young. Would they ever be so happy again?

He looked at the city below: the brook Cedron, the black stone of the city walls and their outworks, the Antonia Fortress and its crenelated towers, the white of the palaces inside the ramparts, and the flat roofs of the houses, so close to one another that they almost formed one single plateau of ocher. Somewhere within was the Galilean.

Lazarus heard the sound of the trumpets announcing the first sacrifices and turned his eyes toward the overwhelming

45

mass of the Temple, which dominated the city. Despite the veil of ashes over his eyes, he could see the enclosures, the colonnades, the courts, the glitter of flawless marble, shining spires and pinnacles, golden pediments and balustrades. Dense plumes of smoke were already rising into the air above the altars. The sound of music of all kinds came from the city: psalms, vibrato singing, the beating of tambourines, hand-clapping, the clashing of cymbals, the deep tones and staccato rhythms of horns, the shrilling of flutes high above the rest. It was the beginning of the Passover rejoicing.

Should he go down into the city now, Lazarus wondered. But he might not find the person he was looking for in all this crowd and excitement. He stood up on weak, unsteady legs, leaning on his staff to keep from falling. Wouldn't it be better to go home to Bethany and come back in a few days? . . . But no—he could not wait.

He entered the Temple square through the Golden Gate and went along the columns of Solomon's Portico. As he had feared, he at once found himself in the midst of a throng. He reached the Court of the Women and made his way among the moneychangers' booths and the stalls of the dove and sparrow sellers, advancing as best he could through the sea of people. Some were listening to discussions between doctors of the Law; others were praying, murmuring with upraised arms. No one moved aside for Lazarus or even seemed to notice him. He did not know whom to approach. He went toward the Court of the Jews and through the Nicador Gate. At the top of the steps, beside the sacred building that was the heart of the Temple, the priests were slaughtering animals for the sacrifice. Lazarus looked down: the blood that had been offered up on the altar now flowed in a continuous stream through channels specially hollowed out in the earth. Tonight the Cedron would run red.

He approached a group of men praying. "Do you know where the Galilean is?" he asked. "The one they call Jesus?"

"Which Galilean?" one of the men answered. "There are thousands of Galileans here."

Lazarus walked on.

"Have you seen the Galilean, the one who gives the blind back their sight?" he asked others.

The people looked at him in amazement. Who was this strange creature with the gray face and breath like ice?

"We're not from Jerusalem," some said, pushing one another in their haste to get away from him.

He went up the three steps that led to the Court of the Priests, passing close by the bleating, bellowing beasts that were tied to eight cedar posts, waiting to be thrust down the incline that led to the sacrificial knife. He was shoved aside by two men pulling a large white sheep.

"Out of the way!" one man yelled at him.

The sheep, slung onto the high marble table and held down, was transfixed through the heart by the keen knife. One last, convulsive spasm, and its seething blood began to run along the grooves carved in the altar. Then the animal was disemboweled, and its entrails were thrown into a brazier.

This sight was familiar to Lazarus, but it now seemed distant and unreal, as if seen in a dream. At that moment the wind blew the smoke from the sacrifices down onto the crowd, and, although he had lost his sense of smell, Lazarus thought he could detect the mingled odor of incense, raw flesh, burning fat, and fresh offal that hung over Jerusalem throughout Passover.

47

"The Galilean who works miracles, is he here? Have you seen him?"

But no one took the trouble to answer. He was ignored, pushed aside, avoided. He left the Temple, certain that he would learn nothing there, and plunged into the labyrinth of narrow streets cut by steps, one or two or whole flights, streets that snaked between the houses toward the Pool of Siloam. Delirium ruled the city. Music, shouting, and laughter rang on all sides. People danced outside brothels. Prostitutes with painted faces and covered with jewelry accosted tipsy Roman soldiers. A group of pilgrims came toward Lazarus singing Passover psalms.

> *When Israel went out of Egypt,*
> *when the house of Jacob*
> *was delivered from the barbarians,*
> *the sea saw it and fled.*

These pilgrims wore the long black robes of the Jews of Babylon. They came from a great distance. There was no point questioning them.

Leaning on his staff and panting, his mouth open, Lazarus reached the teeming district of Sion. He could see bodies prone in alleys and hear the sound of drunken singing and quarreling. Why was he afraid to question the shopkeepers or the peddlers pulling their donkeys laden with tunics, fine linens, carpets, rings and crescents of gold?

A thief, escaping with a purse in his hand, appeared in Lazarus's path. Lazarus did not have time to get out of the way; the man collided with him, and he went sprawling on the cobbles. He heard laughter: children were mocking him. As he got up, one of them threw a handful of pebbles at him.

Not wanting to stay in such narrow, dangerous streets, he made his way toward the Hasmonaean Palace. In the Square of the Fullers, he spoke to two women.

"Do you know the Galilean called Jesus, who works miracles?" he asked.

The women turned their backs on him.

"Just tell me where he is!" Lazarus pleaded.

"We know nothing about him. Go away!" said one of them without turning around.

The sun was high in the sky, and it was hot. Would this shoving and shouting and the hypnotic, thudding music never cease? He should return to Bethany, lie down and rest. His neck hurt, and the light now was so bright, it blinded him. The tall square towers of Herod's fortified palace began to sway before his eyes. Looking up at the ramparts, he could see, dimly through the haze, the golden helmets, red turbans, and long spears of the guards. Perhaps they knew.

But how was he to get in? At the foot of the Phasael Tower, amid a tangle of sticks and crutches, he saw a group of beggars like those who had invaded his courtyard after the miracle. They would be able to tell him.

He went up to them. "Where is Jesus the Galilean, the man who heals the sick?"

"Are you sick?" asked one, eyeing him.

"Yes," said Lazarus. "I want him to cure me."

The beggars exchanged glances.

"He can't cure you or anyone else," said the oldest. "He's a charlatan, a false messiah! He said he would destroy the Temple and rebuild it again in three days."

"Can you give us a little money?" said another, stretching out his hand.

"I have none," said Lazarus. "If I don't find the Galilean, I will soon be one of you. But why do you say he's a false messiah? He gave a blind man back his sight at the Pool of Siloám. I have met him, and I know he performs great miracles."

The man who had asked for money came closer. "You're not one of us. You're too well dressed. You wear a rich man's tunic." And the man seized him roughly by the arm. But, feeling the coldness of the skin, he released him at once and drew back.

"Please tell me where the Galilean is! You can see I'm ill and need him. I believe in him, I know he can help me."

The blind beggar laughed, but answered him. "You'll find him by the Ephraim Gate. Go, if you believe in him. We'll see if he can cure you. But hurry, he won't be there much longer!"

When he reached the dreary, often deserted quarter near the Ephraim Gate, Lazarus saw a crowd of men and women surrounded by a dozen helmeted Roman soldiers armed with spears. The group, advancing slowly, filled the whole street.

They'll delay me, thought Lazarus, who had been walking as fast as he could. I'll get there too late. The Galilean will have gone.

As he drew near them, he heard someone shout, "Save yourself if you can, King of the Jews!" He did not understand what this meant.

Other insults followed. The people—about twenty of them—

seemed excited. Perhaps they were taking a condemned prisoner to Golgotha, the Hill of the Skull. But surely the authorities would not carry out an execution on the thirteenth day of Nisan, the eve of Passover—unless it was a particularly dangerous criminal, a Zealot the Romans wanted to get rid of as soon as possible.

The group came to a halt.

"Let me pass," Lazarus said to the four legionaries who stood shoulder to shoulder, blocking the way. They did not move an inch.

After a pause that seemed an age to Lazarus, the crowd, still shouting, moved on again, but even more slowly than before. Lazarus thought of turning back, or trying another street, but they were now quite near the fortified gate. He could see it in the distance: tall, crenelated, surrounded by three protective walls. What was the Galilean doing in this sinister part of the city? Trying to stop a crucifixion?

When Lazarus reached the top of the last flight of steps before the exit from the city, he saw at last, down below, the one he had been looking for. He stopped in his tracks, refusing at first to believe his eyes.

The Galilean's arms had been tied to the beam that was to serve as the transverse part of his cross. He wore a torn scarlet tunic and staggered as he walked. A circlet woven of thorns had been jammed onto his head like a helmet, making blood run into his hair. Long red wheals showed that he had been scourged until his back was raw. Suddenly a cripple struck at him with his crutch, shouting, "Take that for not curing my leg!"

I am dreaming, thought Lazarus. He had never returned

from his Great Sleep. This insane vision belonged to the realm of the dead.

The crowd moved on. Lazarus hurried down the steps as fast as he could, hunched over his staff, trying to catch up with the crowd. But by the time he reached the street below, they were out of sight.

Why had the Romans condemned him? Was he a Zealot, a thief, a murderer? Perhaps they had mistaken him for someone else, were killing him instead of one of those bandit chiefs who infested the mountains. . . .

He caught up with the legionaries, trembling. How could anyone kill a messiah, a saviour of Israel? He scanned the crowd for the ginger hair of the big man with the goatee, for the fair hair of the young man called John. He saw neither of them: the Galilean's friends had left him to die. No one was going to come to the Galilean's aid!

The trumpets were still sending out their mournful call over ramparts, roofs, and walls; the muffled sound of singing and laughter, cymbals and tambourines still rose from the livelier quarters. The people of Jerusalem, preoccupied, immersed in festive crowds and noise, were not interested today in the commonplace sight of a crucifixion, even the crucifixion of one who had given sight to the blind and raised the dead from their graves.

Fortunately, Lazarus would soon wake, and this fearful vision of a crucified messiah would vanish.

One of the beggars had said that the Galilean had threatened to destroy the Temple. Was that why he had been convicted? But then why would the Romans meddle in something that concerned only the Jews and the Sanhedrin? It made no sense.

"Who will cure *me* if he dies?" Lazarus muttered. "Who will give me back my strength?"

The crowd emerged from the city and moved toward the Hill of the Skull. Lazarus, forgetting how exhausted he was, followed the sinister procession. Now he had a clear view. The Galilean, only ten paces from him, staggered like a drunken man beneath the weight of the beam to which he would be nailed.

A thought struck Lazarus. Of course! The Galilean would set himself free! He was allowing this to happen in order to turn the tables on the Romans and all his enemies. In a moment he would rise up like a great warrior king and smite them all, ridding Israel of its humiliation. Just as in the Song of Solomon, the Messiah would break the pride of the wicked into shards, gather together the chosen people, and lead them into righteousness and peace.

There was no other explanation for what was taking place. Lazarus was about to witness the greatest of all miracles. The power of this man who could bring the dead back to life was so great that he had chosen to establish his kingdom at the very moment his enemies sought to execute him like a thief.

They stripped off his tunic, laid him down naked on his back, and drove nails through his open palms into the crossbeam. The dull thud of each hammer stroke pierced Lazarus as if it were his own hands that were being nailed.

Four of the soldiers lifted the Galilean nailed to the crossbeam. It was raised by ropes attached to the upright, which stood there permanently, a stone's throw from the walls of Jerusalem. Leaving his arms bound to the crossbeam, to prevent their being pulled from their sockets, they hoisted him up slowly. His hands were bleeding. He shrieked with pain. . . . What was he waiting for? Why didn't he set himself free?

Lazarus looked around again for the big man with the goatee and the Galilean's other friends, hoping they were there, with swords hidden under their cloaks, ready to hurl themselves upon the Romans. But all he saw was Haggai, who was watching from a distance.

The soldiers had to make several attempts to hoist the Galilean. They raised and lowered the crossbeam until the two grooves carved in it finally fit on the iron hooks in the upright. Then they nailed his feet, and a Temple servant climbed up a ladder and fixed a wooden board to the top of the cross. On it was written, in three languages, KING OF THE JEWS.

Blood and sweat ran down the Galilean's face; his hair was plastered to his forehead. His body suddenly seemed shorter, thinner. His face was distorted with pain.

Lazarus, drawing nearer, saw that the Galilean was weeping. And then Lazarus really was afraid.

A crucified thief was placed on either side of the Galilean. One of them shouted insults, hurling contempt at a "messiah" who could save not even himself.

It was a long time since the crossbeam had been hoisted into place. The Galilean, his head fallen on his breast, was having more and more difficulty breathing. Lazarus stood motionless, eyes riveted to this body from which the life ebbed. He was losing all hope, and yet he did not leave.

The heat was sweltering. A fierce wind blew the sacrificial

54

smoke down on the Hill of the Skull; the air reeked of it. Near Lazarus, two women in black stood weeping. Why did he not leave this accursed place, where the sight of other bodies, already crucified and cast aside to blacken and decay, reminded him of his own death?

But the Galilean still lived, and Lazarus still wanted to believe a miracle might happen.

The sky had become overcast. Was it near nightfall already? In Bethany, Susannah would be getting anxious. But he could not return to her in the same condition as when he left her. The Galilean had not raised his head or looked at him once. . . .

To lessen the victim's suffering, a soldier fixed a sponge to the end of a pike and dipped it in a mixture of vinegar, incense, and myrrh. When he held it up, the Galilean, almost unconscious, did not see it. The Roman pressed the sponge against his face, and the strong liquid ran down the Galilean's bare heaving breast and belly. Was this what a messiah looked like?

Lazarus, watching, lost all sense of time.

At one point, though he seemed to have stopped breathing, the man on the cross braced his feet and managed to raise himself. His chest began to rise and fall again. The fact that he could do this reassured Lazarus for a moment. The Galilean stayed like that for a while, chest and legs taut. Then he opened his eyes and looked at the handful of people at the foot of the cross. Was he at last going to break free, leap to the ground, and strike down his enemies? He turned painfully from side to side. Lazarus thought he must be looking for his friends. But they all, including the big man with the goatee, had apparently fled in fear, and put walls between themselves and danger. At last the Galilean's eyes, glazing with the approach of death, fell on Lazarus.

Lazarus cried out at once. "I believe in you! You are the Messiah! Escape, and give me back my strength, my life!"

The Galilean seemed not to hear. He let his head fall and collapsed once more.

"You brought me back from the dead! I believe in you!" cried Lazarus.

Limp, bleeding, senseless, the Galilean seemed to have stopped breathing again.

It started to rain. Aside from three soldiers throwing dice, the two women in black, and Lazarus, the onlookers had gone back to the city.

Several times, when he appeared to be dead, the Galilean called upon the prophet Elijah. Toward the ninth hour, as the six ritual trumpet blasts were announcing the beginning of the holiest of days, he uttered a long cry of pain, and his body writhed, as if to free his hands from the nails.

Then once more it rested. The Galilean spoke to one of the women in black at the foot of the cross, but Lazarus could not hear what he said.

The sounds of festivity had long ceased inside the city walls. It was almost dark. Rain still fell, making channels in the ground. But Lazarus did not move.

One of the soldiers, taking a club, broke the legs of the two crucified thieves; they had been dead for a long time.

Lazarus heard the bones crack. Then the Roman climbed up a ladder and drove his sword into the Galilean's breast. After that, they took him down from the cross, passing ropes under his arms and pulling his hands free and then his feet. The flesh was torn because of the nails.

They let the broken body fall into the mud. One of the women in black rushed forward and, wailing, took the rain-soaked corpse in her arms.

Only then did Lazarus realize that it was over.

After waiting to see the Galilean's body laid in a tomb at the foot of Golgotha, Lazarus went away slowly, aimlessly. He climbed back up toward the Antonia Fortress. Night had fallen, but the rain stopped. He made his way to the pool with five columns. He no longer thought of Susannah and his sisters, who must be waiting for him, but moved in a kind of fog, trying to get as far as possible from the Hill of the Skull, from that place of death.

He walked, paying no attention to anything, not knowing where he was or where he was going. He climbed a barren slope dotted with scrub and realized he did not know the place; but that did not matter. He could feel the texture of the soil change gradually as he walked, and before long the ground around him was quite bare.

When his legs refused to carry him any farther, he wrapped himself in his cloak and lay down on his side. And he who had forgotten what sleep was fell quickly into a state that closely resembled it. He lay curled up, exhausted. Every so often the cold roused him vaguely from his torpor, and he sensed that he was surrounded by countless obscure noises.

The cry of an animal made him start, and he tried to sit up, but a pain in the back of the neck forced him to lie still again. All he could see was the gray-blue darkness above. Then he remembered a cross, a crown of thorns, a torn and bloody hand, a lifeless body in the mud. . . . His teeth chattered.

Next morning, the heat of the sun forced him back to consciousness. Goaded by flies and mosquitoes, he dragged himself to an opening in the rock higher up the hill. It was a shallow recess, offering protection from the light and the scorching rays of the sun. He could no longer see the walls of Jerusalem. What was he doing out here so near the desert?

He stayed curled in his shelter until noon.

He thought constantly about the Galilean. He could see him clearly in his mind's eye: bound, nailed, weeping, crying out in pain on the cross. No attempt to defend himself or escape. The man had let himself be scourged, humiliated, crucified. How could Lazarus ever have taken him for the Messiah?

And yet he *had* brought him back from the grave. Even if he had not really restored him to life, he had waken him from the Great Sleep.

And now the Galilean, too, lay in a tomb, suspended in a bottomless pit.

"A messiah cannot die," Lazarus muttered. "The Almighty sends him down to earth to make His cause triumph, to wreak vengeance on the enemies of Israel, to restore glory to His chosen people."

The man had been only a magician, a beggar. . . .

The sun rose in the sky; as it pursued its course, its fierce light crept nearer to Lazarus in his shallow cave. Lazarus's head pounded. The sand outside became so white, he could not bear to look at it. He heard the hiss of a snake. He would have to return to Bethany, even if it meant appearing to Susannah and his sisters unchanged.

And yet, when the Galilean brought him back to life, had he not intended it to show that he came from the Most High and derived his power from Him alone? Who but the Messiah, the emissary of God, could raise the dead? That was not the trick of a mere magician. . . . But why this pitiful end? Why had he not given Lazarus back his youth and strength and beauty, so that all who saw the miracle would know its greatness?

What if he had been only a prophet, like Elisha or Elijah, whom he had called upon when he felt his end was near? This possibility terrified Lazarus, for it meant that the Galilean was nothing more than a man, who, by dying, had abandoned Lazarus to his fate, his suffering, his non-life.

No, a miracle as great as my awakening, he kept telling himself, can come only from God Himself. He knows I have always feared and honored Him. I came back through His will, and He will not forget me.

It was not until the eighth hour that he got back to Bethany. Susannah, who had been standing on the roof since sunrise, waiting, consumed by anxiety, saw him in the distance limping along the road. Torn between joy at his return and sorrow on realizing that he could not have found the Galilean, she hesitated to run out to meet him. She had so hoped that he would be cured! There he was, leaning on his staff, stooped, ashen-faced, just as on the morning of his departure. Disappointment kept her from hurrying to him. From the roof she watched his painful approach.

The Passover dancing in the street broke up as he drew near. People fell back to let him pass: they were afraid of him. She had to admit to herself that, lying beside him at night, she often felt an irrational fear, brief but overwhelming.

The dance started again behind him; the flutes and tambourines began to play once more. He stumbled and nearly fell. His clothes were stained with mud, his face drawn with pain. He could not walk straight, and his legs almost gave way at every step. Why did she not go and help him?

At last, when he entered the courtyard, she brought herself to go downstairs to greet him. She went to kiss him, but the dank air around him made her hold back. She looked at his bloodless lips, and suddenly was filled with disgust, a disgust that only the filthiest objects could inspire. But she overcame this unworthy, irrational reaction, and took his arm. His skin was cold as ice beneath his damp cloak.

"I've been so frightened," she said. "Why didn't you come back last evening? You could have looked for the Galilean again this morning. Your sisters and I were worried!"

He was too short of breath to answer. He had to lean on her to climb to the upper room. As they stood by the bed, she removed his cloak and tunic. His body, naked and shivering, no longer repelled her, thank God. What had come over her? She was ashamed of her momentary weakness. He complained of the cold, so she wrapped him in a thick blanket. He lay down slowly, cautiously, as if afraid that he might break. She noticed that the skin on his feet was torn, shredded, and was surprised there was no bleeding.

She sat down beside him. His eyes remained wide open, staring. She reproached herself for having let him go alone.

60

Next time, she would go with him, whether he liked it or not, and together they would find the man he was seeking, even if they had to cross the desert, even if they had to go as far as Tyre.

Martha and Mary knew by now of their brother's return and hastened up to see him. Dismayed to find that he had not been cured, they asked him what had happened. Everyone said that the Galilean was still in Jerusalem. Three days ago, a peddler had seen him overturn the tables of the money-changers in the Temple, in the Court of the Gentiles, near the columns of Solomon's Portico.

Lazarus, after a long silence, began to describe what he had witnessed. He told of the crown of thorns and of how the Galilean's arms had been tied to the crossbeam, of the clothes torn off, the hands pierced by nails, the beam raised. He told of the thief shrieking his hatred and contempt and of the tears and cries of pain, the sponge lifted up on the pike, the rain, the two women in black, the crying out to Elijah, the sword thrust into the already darkening breast.

"He did nothing to save himself," he said. "He submitted to a miserable death. He was not the Messiah. He could not do anything for me. He was only a prophet, or a beggar. . . ."

The three women listened, incredulous.

"From now on I will go and beg every day at the gates of Jerusalem," he said, "and pray in the Temple, until the Almighty, who alone decided that I should rise from the grave, consents to help me."

In Jerusalem, at dawn on the day after Passover, a Temple guard burst into Haggai's house and told him that during the night persons unknown had rolled away the stone at the entrance to the Galilean's tomb and removed the body.

"Impossible!" cried the priest. "Caiaphas and I persuaded the procurator to post armed sentries there. We heard him give the order."

"Well, the tomb is empty now," said the guard. "The Romans were asleep and saw nothing. Some women are already saying that the Galilean has risen from the dead."

So, what Haggai had feared had actually happened! He must act quickly to stop the rumor from spreading.

"Who are these women?" he asked.

"A prostitute by the name of Mary Magdalene. Abigail, the daughter of Alphaeus. And Mary, the mother of James."

"They must be arrested at once, before they have time to speak."

"They left an hour ago, declaring there had been a miracle. One of them has entered Jerusalem, another is on her way to Emmaus, and the third is making for Bethany."

Haggai set out immediately for the Hill of the Skull. He could not believe that the handful of beggars who had accompanied the Galilean up to the time of his arrest had been able to elude the sentries, roll away the stone, and remove the body from under their very noses. It was impossible. Unless . . . Had not this Jesus of Nazareth said that he would come to life again after three days? And did not the Book of Deuteronomy foretell the resurrection of the Messiah on the third day after his death? But no—he must not think like that. He must avoid doubt at all costs!

Reaching the foot of Golgotha, Haggai saw the open tomb and the stone rolled to one side. A crowd had already gathered.

He went to the entrance of the tomb and stood at the top of the dark stairway. He remembered Lazarus's ashen face and icy breath, the smell of earth about his clothes and skin. A shiver ran down Haggai's spine. He descended the rough steps hewn in the rock. With apprehension, he followed the narrow passage that led to the funeral chamber.

The odor of incense and aloes still hovered between the close, cold walls. When his eyes adjusted to the dark, he could see the shroud lying discarded on the stone edge of the tomb. The bandages that had been wrapped around the dead man's hands and feet trailed loose on the ground. He picked up one of these strips of cloth, but dropped it quickly when he found it sticky with blood. Why had the thieves removed the bandages? Would it not have been easier to carry the body away as it was? They must have been very sure of themselves, to take their time like that!

The priest left the tomb and questioned the soldiers. "What happened? You were supposed to be guarding this place!"

"We were asleep and saw nothing," one of them said.

"Impossible," said Haggai. "No one could have moved that stone without waking you."

"It was like that at dawn. The body was gone."

"The procurator will have you punished for negligence. I'll see to that myself!"

"Pilate went back to Caesarea first thing this morning." It was the decurion who spoke. "He didn't seem to think the matter was very serious."

"Then he's making a mistake!" cried Haggai. "A big mistake! This agitator proclaimed himself king of the Jews; he challenged the authority of Caesar. His disappearance will cause unrest, riots among the people. It will endanger Rome.

. . . We'll tell the propraetor of Syria that beggars came and stole the body. Jesus was a usurper. We warned Pilate, and now he must accept the responsibility."

The Sanhedrin met just before noon. Most of its members had been in that same chamber of polished stone behind the Temple three days before, when they sentenced the Galilean to death. They took their places again on the stone benches arranged around the chair of Caiaphas, the high priest. As before, they were dressed in their black cloaks and had long white scarves around their necks and traditional kaffiyehs on their heads. They all noted the absence of Nicodemus, who had been the accused's most passionate defender during the trial.

Haggai, still agitated, was the first to speak. Since everyone knew what had happened during the night, he did not detail it. Instead, he confined himself to insisting that the Temple guards be sent off at once in search of the thieves.

Although all the Sadducees seemed to agree with this, he could hear murmurs of disapproval from some of the Pharisees, and in particular from Bartholomew, a friend of Nicodemus. Haggai turned toward Caiaphas to get his reaction, but the high priest, who was listening slumped in his chair with his eyes shut, remained silent, slowly combing his bushy beard with his fingers. He seemed to be bored with the whole affair.

So Haggai addressed Joseph of Arimathaea. "Is it true that the tomb in which the Galilean was laid belongs to you?"

"Yes," answered Joseph, appearing unconcerned.

"Was it you who had the body removed?"

"Although I never heard the man in question say anything more than what has already been said by the prophets, and although I don't share the hatred that many here—and you in particular—feel toward him, I bowed, as always, to the decision of the Council. I lent him my tomb, nothing more. So that his body would not stay nailed to the cross during Passover. He was a beggar, who possessed nothing in the world, and I did not think it right for him to rot on the ground with the carcasses of murderers and thieves. Of what happened during the night I know nothing, and, frankly, I think it ridiculous to make all this fuss. As if we had anything to fear from a dead man!"

"People are saying he's risen from the dead!" cried Elihu.

"That's nonsense," said Bartholomew.

"But many believe it and are spreading it around," Haggai went on. "We had sense enough to condemn the blasphemer. In doing that, we were only carrying out the Law. But if we allow rumors of his so-called resurrection to circulate, we'll be in worse danger than if we had let him live."

"We shouldn't have sentenced him to death, then!" said Bartholomew.

"What's done is done!" exclaimed Haggai, standing. "We know that some whisper that he is the son of God, though most in Jerusalem regard him as a madman and a usurper. It isn't difficult to imagine what will happen if we don't find the body. The people badly need a messiah."

"But they expect a king, a warrior, another David," said Joseph of Arimathaea quietly. "And he kept saying that his kingdom was not of this world. You know that everyone abandoned him. Who believes in him now?"

"You forget that he performed miracles," observed Samuel,

the oldest and most respected member of the Sanhedrin, who sat on Caiaphas's right. "Thirty-seven miracles! He performed them everywhere—not only here in Jerusalem, but in Samaria and Galilee, too. I never heard of so many marvels in all my life: he gave sight to people blind from birth, made the dumb speak, restored to cripples the use of their legs and arms, delivered those possessed by evil spirits. He even brought a dead man forth from the grave in Bethany—we've discussed that incident at length here."

"That resurrection was never proved!" shouted a scribe.

"The one among us who saw Lazarus son of Chaim afterward has no doubt about it," said the old man slowly. "And all on whom the Galilean performed miracles will testify in his favor. They are irrefutable proof of his power."

There was a brief silence. Haggai looked at Samuel, at his strong nose and long white beard. Samuel's influence over Caiaphas was great.

"The fact that he performed miracles doesn't prove he was the Messiah," said Bartholomew.

"The coming of the Messiah lies at the heart of our religion," said Haggai, turning toward the high priest. "Why must the liberator of Israel be another Solomon or David? God might very well choose the son of a carpenter from Nazareth. Wasn't David himself a shepherd? No one can say in what way God will come to the aid of his people. You are right, Samuel—the miracles of Jesus may undermine weaker spirits."

"You talk as though you yourself believed he was the Messiah!" mocked Bartholomew.

At this, many of the Sadducees rose to their feet.

"I believe no such thing!" replied Haggai.

"Are you sure?" asked Joseph of Arimathaea, smiling. "Didn't you swear to us that he brought Lazarus back from the Great Sleep?"

"That was only a magic trick inspired by the devil!" cried Hillel.

"A magician cannot raise the dead!"

"The Galilean never raised the dead!"

"It's you who have been taken in by the miracles, you who are one of the weaker spirits, you who believe the Galilean is the Messiah!" Zerah accused Bartholomew.

"What bothers you," replied Bartholomew, "is the way he criticized our affluence and our hypocrisy!"

"Speak for yourself! It was you Pharisees he was criticizing!"

Caiaphas opened his eyes at last. "Stop this childish squabbling!" he said in a strong voice. Straightening his heavy body, he turned toward Samuel, then regarded all the other members of the Sanhedrin as they stood facing him.

"The Galilean's power must be great indeed," Caiaphas sighed, "if we almost come to blows over him." Then, gravely: "You are wrong, Haggai. The Scriptures tell us that the Messiah will come as a king. Was this man a king? . . . No. He was a beggar, a blasphemer, and that was why we condemned him to death. There was no truth in him great enough to make the people of Israel renounce the teaching of two thousand years. They would not imperil themselves for the sake of a rumored resurrection. We had the Romans crucify him. Let that be the end of the matter."

Haggai made as if to speak, but the high priest stopped him with a gesture.

"If we go looking for the body and those who stole it,"

Caiaphas continued, "it will appear that we are afraid of him, and then people really will take him for the Messiah. Our best course is to do nothing. The absurd rumor of a resurrection will die out of its own accord, and the false prophet will be forgotten. . . . I'm an old man, but this business has worried me profoundly. Why such passion among you all of a sudden? We have known other false messiahs. . . . Three days ago, in this very room, we were at odds over this same man, and today Master Nicodemus refused to attend the Council meeting—an unheard-of state of affairs! How can we have been reduced to such dissension and ill-feeling by a mere beggar, a half-magician who blasphemed that he was the son of God?

"I do not want to hear the matter mentioned again! Jesus the Galilean is dead. He was not the Messiah. No one is going to look for his body. He was nothing. We do not need to bother about him."

Haggai left the Temple convinced that Caiaphas had just made an irreparable mistake. On his way home he even thought of sending the guards to look for the thieves himself. But could he really do such a thing? Strong as his position was in the Sanhedrin, it would be dangerous for him to defy the high priest's orders so openly.

At home, frowning, he passed Elizabeth, his wife, without looking at her. In the inner courtyard, the table had been set by the maidservant for the midday meal. The shewbread and slices of mutton, leftovers from the Passover sacrifices in the Temple, were waiting for him there. It was now well past noon, yet he was not hungry. He wanted to go straight up to

68

the room he used for study and prayer, but Yona, his daughter, called out to him impatiently to come and bless the meal. She was ravenous. Absently Haggai took off his cloak and white scarf and reclined on the divan facing her. The rumor of resurrection by now must be spreading through Judea, and would soon reach Samaria. It was too late to stop it. The best thing he could do was forget it.

Elizabeth came and took her place beside him. He bowed his head and recited verses asking the Almighty to bless their food that day. He broke the bread in silence and handed it around, then poured wine into his cup and drank deeply. Again he pondered the threat that the false rumor presented to Israel. Could it really shake the fundamental principles of the faith? Or was he exaggerating the danger?

Haggai took three slices of mutton, put one on the silver plate in front of his wife, one on the plate of his daughter, and the third on his own.

What he feared most was that the mere idea of a resurrected messiah might provoke a revolt against the Romans. The slightest thing was enough to stir up the people of Israel, ever ready to turn against the invader. The procurator had been hostile ever since Tiberius failed to back him up in the business of the shields, and was only waiting for a chance to get even. It was not hard to imagine what his response would be if there was trouble. Golgotha would bristle with crosses again; repression, more outrages; yet another escalation of hatred and violence. The end of Israel's freedom to practice a religion which the invader could not understand and barely tolerated. The end of the delicate balance of power achieved only by the patient efforts of the Sadducees. Pilate would be more than happy to silence what he regarded as a race of fanatics, and this time, if there was bloodshed, Tiberius, fed up with the problems of a tiny, remote province that consisted largely of desert, would not rein his representative. The Sanhedrin would lose whatever influence it still had; the heathens would enter the Temple and there set up an effigy of their emperor.

Admittedly, thought Haggai as he fingered the thin slice of meat, the Galilean had not spoken against Rome. On the contrary, he told the people to pay Caesar his dues. Nor had he preached anything but what was already written in the Scriptures. But he had preached too vehemently, as if the purpose of the Scriptures was to challenge the established order, the only possible order, which preserved Israel.

Elizabeth, seeing her husband so gloomy, asked him what had happened in the Sanhedrin.

"Nothing," he answered. "No action will be taken. It is already too late to stop the rumor of resurrection. Caiaphas doesn't realize the danger we're in, and I could not persuade him to act."

Then Samuel's words came back into his mind, about the many marvels performed, the miracles. It was true that each of those miracles was proof that the Galilean possessed some supernatural power. They could persuade doubters, rouse believers to fanaticism.

There was Jair, the blind man at the Pool of Siloam whose sight had been restored. And, above all, Lazarus, in his house in Bethany, with his fleshless body and the smell of damp earth still on him.

Haggai remembered Lazarus, also, in the rain, leaning on his staff at the foot of the cross. Lazarus alone had followed Jesus of Nazareth to the end, when everyone else abandoned him, when none of his followers and friends dared show themselves on Golgotha. Despite the physical suffering that could easily be imagined, Lazarus had stood in the rain for hours by the man dying in agony. Such courage and determination proved that Lazarus believed the Galilean was the Messiah.

Suddenly, Haggai realized what a threat Lazarus was: here was evidence in support of the most extraordinary of all the Galilean's miracles, the miracle of raising himself from his own Sleep. Lazarus would not hesitate to present himself as proof that Jesus was the son of God. . . .

Haggai asked himself if it would not be best for Lazarus to be removed.

He looked at his daughter reclining on the other side of the table. Beneath her saffron gown he could see the curve of her breasts. It would soon be time to find her a husband. . . . She noticed his appraisal and lowered her eyes. Was it right, in her presence, to decide on a man's death? And what if the Galilean really was the Messiah? It would be unthinkable then to do away with a proof of his divinity. What Haggai had said to the high priest was perfectly true: it was possible for God to choose a carpenter's son. And—there was no doubt about it—Lazarus *had* returned from the Great Sleep.

The idea of a messiah allowing himself to die in order to rise again in three days was not that absurd. But even if it was true, thought Haggai, trying to reassure himself, it would not matter whether Lazarus was alive or dead. The advent of the Kingdom would not depend on Lazarus.

Haggai sighed. If he had not gone to Bethany, he would not be asking himself all these questions.

As soon as he finished eating, he left the table, went upstairs, walked around the balcony of the inner courtyard, and shut himself in his room, to study a transcription of the three statements to be used as evidence against Tirzah, the adulterous wife of Arcan who was to be tried by the Council the next day.

But Lazarus haunted him. Haggai could still hear his hoarse breathing. It was almost as if he were actually in the room. Lazarus, who would make people believe that the Galilean had supernatural powers. . . .

Imprisoning him was one possibility, but that involved risks. It was bound to leak out in Jerusalem that the man raised from the dead in Bethany was being held. Which would make it difficult for Haggai to claim that the memory of the Galilean held no fears for him. The situation would turn against him and against the Sanhedrin, of which he was one of the most prominent members.

No, the only way to remove Lazarus and the threat he represented was to have him killed. Let the murder be regarded as the work of some bandit. There were bandits enough in the hills around Jerusalem.

He finished his work at the eighth hour. Then, with arms upraised and his prayer shawl over his head and shoulders, he prayed at length to the Almighty to guide him in his decision.

The danger of uprisings, massacres, and destruction inclined him to order Lazarus's death. But the prospect of murder, which was against the Law and all the teaching of the Scriptures, repelled him. Condemning to death, together with the seventy members of the Council, a false prophet and blasphemer—that had been a collective act that had nothing in common with this solitary decision, for which he would have to bear the whole responsibility forever.

Toward the eleventh hour, Haggai thought of going to his friend Zerah for advice. But Zerah was impulsive and sometimes hasty in his judgments. He would not be able to shed the light that Haggai needed.

Time was short. Soon people would seek out the miracle of Bethany, and the resurrected Lazarus would be exhibited everywhere, making all believe in Jesus of Nazareth. If he himself, a priest and an influential member of the Sanhedrin, had been troubled by Lazarus, what would be the reaction of the naïve and gullible?

The problem was no longer whether or not the Galilean had risen from the dead. The problem was quite different. It involved the defense of Israel and of Israel's religion.

When the sky over Jerusalem was dotted with the brilliance of innumerable stars, Haggai sent for his servant Matthew and instructed him to go to Bethany and kill Lazarus.

Lazarus dreaded the night. As the light faded, as dusk fell, his anguish increased. He hated lying awake in the dark for endless hours, alone with his fears. Even sharp physical pain was preferable, for pain was a sign of life; pain might prove that he still existed.

Since his return from Jerusalem, he kept seeing the crown of thorns, the bleeding brow, the torn hands. Death was continually on his mind, the bottomless pit into which he longed to vanish once more. He tried to remember the darkness, the eternal void without incident or sorrow, but could not recover that feeling of hovering absence.

Often he would go up on the roof and stare down at the dim courtyard below. It drew him. Sooner or later, he would throw himself off some height and be dashed to pieces on the hard ground. He would go back to Jerusalem, to its towers, just for that.

If only he could stop thinking!

He tried to pray. In his room, for hours, he would prostrate himself, stretch out his arms, shut his eyes. But no words would come. He had forgotten how to speak to God, and was no longer certain, even, that there was any point in asking for His help.

The people of Bethany were saying that the Galilean had risen from the dead. But Lazarus felt no inclination to try to find him. Was it really credible that the Galilean had let himself be crucified only to come back to life three days later? That did not make sense.

For three nights he lay awake beside the sleeping Susannah, waiting for the dawn, his eyes fixed on the open square of the window. It seemed the night would never end, the troubled night that was so unlike the peaceful dark of the Great Sleep.

He no longer rebelled, he had given up. Everything left him indifferent, everything except the pale and joyless streak of light that finally reached the foot of the bed. He no longer had any desire, any will. All he wanted was to go to sleep forever.

On the fourth morning after the man from Galilee was crucified, Lazarus got up before daybreak. Barefoot and without his cloak, he went down the stairs and out into the darkness, walked along the main street between the sleeping houses, not noticing the cold. He felt no pain when he stepped on a sharp stone. At least, he thought, I won't suffer when I hurl myself from the walls of Jerusalem.

For Susannah's sake, too, it was best for him to die. The

previous evening, he had noticed the dread in her eyes when he lay down beside her.

As he passed Eliphas's house, he resolved to speak to him that very day. The carpenter shop must open again. Saul still waited for his chest and Daniel for his lintels. Eliphas would share his earnings with Susannah, Martha, and Mary. That way, they would be fed and clothed after Lazarus was gone.

Hearing a noise behind him, he turned. Everything happened very quickly. The shape of a man rushed toward him. A terrible weight fell on his shoulders and knocked him to the ground. Something sharp was thrust under his arm, between his ribs, though he felt no pain. He struggled to get up, to escape, but the weapon struck again, this time in his stomach. He drew his legs up for protection and could feel hot breath on the back of his neck. Shielding his face with his arms, he felt what seemed to be innumerable insects swarming over his body.

The attacker, grunting, caught hold of his wrist, twisting it away from his face. The sharp object cut a third time, in the neck, below his ear, with disconcerting ease. Then the heavy dark form abruptly rose and fled.

The insects trilled inside Lazarus's head, and ran over his forehead and among the roots of his hair. The sound they made was unbearable. They entered his bones. Thousands of darts pricked at his cheeks, his chest, his back.

At last he saw the opening of a well at his feet. Through dark mist he edged toward it. The pricking abated. He dragged himself nearer. A gentle, boundless warmth pervaded him. He recognized that warmth. Now he remembered.

It was as if he were waking up, though he knew that he had not been asleep. A blur of mauve formed above the hills. Dawn. He tried to remember the warmth and the well, the dark opening. But the gentleness that had enveloped him was gone.

He started to move, first his arms and then his legs. He tried to find the pain, the place that hurt, but there was no pain. All he could feel was the weight of his body and a certain thickness around his bones. The insects no longer swarmed, the pricking had ceased. He shut his eyes, desperately searching for the way to the bottomless pit.

Surely he could not have lost it, after being so close!

Raising himself slightly, he saw that his tunic was torn over his stomach and under the arm. The man had fallen on him and struck him in three places. Cautiously, he felt his side and, without looking, located the gaping cut. His fingers explored its depth. How could he still be alive with such a wound? He looked at his hand. No blood. He touched the gash on his neck. It, too, was dry. Looking down at his stomach, he almost fainted: it lay horribly wide open, exposing layers of gray tissue. That blow alone was enough to have killed him. He felt his neck again: that, too, was a mortal wound.

"And yet I am alive," he murmured. "I was killed, but can still see and move and think!"

He got to his feet and made for home, to call Martha and Susannah, but he stopped in the courtyard, outside the door, suddenly remembering the time he had cut himself on the saw in his workshop. That cut had not bled, either.

He began to understand what this meant. He no longer

had any life to lose. He had emerged from the Great Sleep and would never be able to return to it.

In the days that followed, Lazarus withdrew deeper into himself. He asked Martha to put a linen curtain around his bed, and lay behind it for days at a time without seeing anyone or being seen.

He was shocked, confused by what had happened to him.

In the past, his dearest wish had been that he might never die. Not once had he thought about what not dying really implied. It had nothing to do with life; such a boundless eternity was the very opposite of life.

He kept fingering his wounds, no longer surprised that they had not killed him. Apart from the mysterious attack—probably the work of a robber—everything that had happened since he emerged from the tomb hung together quite logically. As soon as he "awoke" and found himself with a half-decomposed body, the clammy, evil-smelling gray skin of a corpse, and wounds that did not bleed, he ought to have realized that he would never return to his Great Sleep.

It was necessary and right that every life should end sooner or later. Deprived of its inevitable end, he suddenly saw, existence lost all meaning. Only the certainty that time was limited made people act, use each hour for a definite purpose, and strive to get the most out of every day, every opportunity, every happiness, as if each was unique and would never come again.

Living forever meant the end of life's desires, life's struggles and risks; it meant knowing neither sorrow nor joy, a joy that was all the greater for being brief. How could anyone conceive of a world of immortal beings? They would be incapable of fighting for anything, they would have no faith or fear of God, no needs, wants, or feelings.

Immortality was a featureless horizon: it was death.

And he, Lazarus, was doomed to live forever! He could not believe that a punishment so cruel had been reserved for him.

So he lay on his bed behind the linen curtain, motionless, day after day. Sometimes he would be overcome with rage against his fate and against the inhuman God who had decreed it. He would sit up and shout his defiance, that he wanted to live, that he had done nothing wrong, but then he would sink back again into helpless anguish.

Susannah came up from time to time with a little food, but he refused to touch it. She did not know what to say; when she tried to speak to him, he did not answer. When she sometimes looked behind the curtain, she would see him lying motionless with his eyes wide open.

He was worse since the morning he came home with those three revolting wounds. Who could have attacked him like that? They looked like knife wounds. She had tried to dress them, but he had pushed her away. And the wounds had remained the same—not bleeding, not oozing, but not healing, either.

Susannah was afraid to go near him. His body, his breath seemed colder, more repugnant than ever. She no longer wanted him at her side at night, but did not dare say so.

She still lay down near him every evening, in the light nightdress that left her bosom and shoulders bare. She told herself that he was suffering so much already, it would be wrong to do anything that might increase his loneliness and misery.

She told herself that she loved him as much as ever.

One night, seeing him so silent and withdrawn, she drew close and forced herself to put her arms around him.

Lazarus was aware of her softness, her warmth. He turned toward her. But she did not smile. Instead, her face wore an expression of sorrow. . . . She was young and beautiful, but he did not desire her. Once, he thought, she opened her legs for me every night. But now he needed nothing, not her body, not her love, and it would be that way forever. He would watch her grow old. Day after day, he would see her change, her hair turn gray, then white, her slim figure thicken, her bosom sag, the face that was now so smooth grow wrinkled. Furrows would appear on her neck and gnarled blue veins on her legs. Until at last she died, while he watched, and left him for the Great Sleep.

And then one day she would become so distant a memory that he would not even remember her face and body.

How sorry he was that he had not paid more attention to her before! He had loved her, and desired her, of course, from that very first morning he went to make some repairs for her father on the other side of Bethany and saw her run from the house laughing. But he realized now that he had always thought of her as a child.

"I never spoke to you about anything serious," he said.

She looked at him in surprise.

But he could sense her tension, her distance, even, though her arms were still around him. He moved away. "I know you're afraid of me. The way you watch me when you think I'm not looking. You probably would prefer not to stay with me at night."

She met his eyes for a moment, then hung her head without answering.

For over a week now, Martha had been obliged to earn some money by going every other morning to the valley of the Jordan, a five-hour walk from Bethany. There, with her bare hands, she collected clay from the riverbank, and brought two large bagfuls back on her donkey after nightfall. The next morning, she would go to Jerusalem, to sell her load for a few coins to the potters there.

Thus, she finally heard the rumor that was circulating in the lower part of the city. It was being whispered, like a secret, that the Galilean who had died on the cross was the son of God, that he had risen from the dead, and that some people had seen and spoken to him near Emmaus.

Martha inquired further, but those who believed the rumor were reluctant to give particulars. They seemed to want to remain anonymous.

At last an old man answered her questions. Yes, the Galilean had come back to life; the soldiers found his tomb empty three days after his death.

"I never doubted he was the son of God," he said. "He performed all kinds of miracles to prove it. But even before we learned that he could cure the blind and the lame, many of us suspected that he was the son of God."

She questioned people in the upper city, near the Temple,

but they laughed in her face and said that it was all nonsense. Everyone knew the Galilean's body had been taken away by robbers.

"I saw him go by in the street outside my house," said one young man. "The bar of his cross was tied to his back, and the thorns had been crushed down on his head. He could hardly walk. His face was covered with blood. It was pitiful. He was like any other prisoner on his way to be crucified, only more wretched than most. I was quite close, I could see him weeping. The people who say he is a god must be liars, or idiots."

"Many believe in him!"

The man shrugged. "There'll never be a shortage of idiots."

Martha went up to Lazarus's room that evening to tell him about the rumor.

"I know they say he's risen from the dead," Lazarus replied. "But it's not true."

Yet, although for the past two or three days he had sunk into a deep lethargy, on the morning after Martha spoke to him he was once more agitated by the doubts that had haunted him before.

He looked around him. His bare white room. How long had he been lying there inert? How much of his own eternity had it taken up? Again the image of the torn hands was before him, and of the limp body hitting the mud.

"Why do you pursue me?" he muttered. "Why do you not leave me in peace? Haven't you done enough to me? Why must I keep thinking about you?"

Martha seemed convinced. . . . But Martha would believe anything. Still, her certainty worried Lazarus.

But why, if the Galilean was the son of God, would his Father have let them crucify him? Why would He have let His own son be sacrificed? For what purpose?

Lazarus buried his head in the pillow and put his hands over his ears. He did not want to think anymore, either about the Galilean or about his own fate!

Yet, if he stayed in bed, troubled by visions and asking himself questions to which there were no answers, he would never have the chance to find out the truth, to understand the incredible thing that had happened to him. He sat up. He could not tell whether it was raining or if the sun was shining outside, for everything looked gray in the square of the window. And the chest, the walls, the mud floor. . . . No, he would not make this room his sepulcher. The truth must exist somewhere, and he must try to find it.

That evening, he went out, for the first time since he was attacked nearly three weeks earlier. He went to Eliphas and told him to open the carpenter shop the following day. "You can come and work at my place," he said to his former apprentice, "and use my tools and bench. In return, give half of whatever money you earn to my wife and sisters until I come back."

At home, he waited until the three women went to bed, then stood near Susannah as she slept. She was lying facedown, her curly hair fallen over her bare shoulders. One arm lay outside the blanket, her fingers touching the pillow on which her head rested. He bent, brushed his cheek against her hand. The hand of a child. She gave a little sigh, and he moved away, afraid of waking her. Her full red lips reminded him of their embraces, when once he had held her in his powerful arms, moving between her thighs slowly so that his desire would not end too soon. The memory belonged to another world, a world that was far away. Another life . . .

And what if he never came back? Perhaps he should divorce her before he left, so that she could marry again, find a man who would be able to love her and give her a son.

No. There was no time for that. Every minute counted now. He brought his cold lips as close as he could to the white nape of her neck, between two locks of hair.

Then, tying a cloth around his own neck to hide its open wound, he took his cloak and staff and left the village unseen, setting off in the solitude and darkness on his long quest through time.

TWO

It was a long way to Emmaus, and Lazarus didn't enter Cleopas the blacksmith's forge until dusk was settling over the hills.

Cleopas, still at work, sat at his anvil in his leather apron, his bare chest and arms ruddy from the glow of the fire. He was so absorbed in what he was doing, so deafened by the rhythmic thud of his hammer on the red-hot point of the plowshare he was making, that he neither saw nor heard his visitor's approach. Before speaking to him, Lazarus watched for a moment. In the stifling heat of the workshop, the smith's muscles glistened with sweat and swelled as he brought the hammer down again and again on the triangle of incandescent metal, each time leaving it flatter and sharper. Lazarus envied the man his strength.

When Cleopas paused in his work, the silence was great. He gripped the blade firmly in a long pair of tongs.

"I wish to talk to you," said Lazarus. "I've come all the way from Jerusalem to see you."

The smith turned, surprised. "Who are you?" he asked.

"I am Lazarus, son of Chaim, whom the Galilean raised from the dead in Bethany. You must have heard of me."

The smith looked at the gaunt, cracked face, hideous in the flickering light of the forge. He frowned. "What do you want?"

"They told me at the inn that you met Jesus of Nazareth the day after Passover, three days after his death. I want to know what the Galilean said to you and what he looked like when he was here."

Cleopas, who had not put down his tongs, said nothing. He stared at Lazarus.

"You can see that I have returned from the Great Sleep. . . . Surely you know my story."

"I've heard of you," said the smith, not taking his eyes off Lazarus.

"Please, tell me about your meeting with the Galilean."

"If he brought you back to life, he must have been your friend, so you ought to know more about him than I do. Why do you come and ask me?"

"I know nothing. I haven't seen him since he died on the cross."

"It will be dark soon, and I haven't finished my work. . . . Why should I talk? No one believes me when I tell what happened. They make fun of me, they say I was drunk that evening."

"I'll believe you!" said Lazarus. "Look, my skin is the skin of a corpse; I smell of earth, corruption. Who but the Galilean could have brought me back from the dead? I know that anything is possible. Whatever you tell me, no matter how incredible, I will believe it."

Cleopas turned back to the forge. "I've let my fire go out, listening to you." He put down the tongs and stood up. He was a head taller than Lazarus. Pushing a large pair of bellows in under the stone hood of the forge, he worked them with such force, the turf immediately reddened again. "How do I know you won't leave here and go straight to the inn, where for a cup of wine you'll tell everyone in the village what I've said, and start them all laughing at me again?"

"I don't drink anymore," said Lazarus. "Hunger and thirst have left me. And I never sleep. I have no desires, no needs. It's worse than death."

"Why did the Galilean bring you back to life, then?"

"I don't know. I came here because I'm trying to find out."

Cleopas shook his head and was silent for a while. Then he worked the bellows again, until a shower of red sparks flew up.

"I met him on the road to Jerusalem," Cleopas said at last. "I was with my brother, Philip. I believed in him, because of all the things I'd heard about him. The miracles and so on. Of course, I had never set eyes on him before, so anyone could have pretended to be him. . . . And I'd heard what had happened three days before, on the Hill of the Skull, and I was sorry. I'd been so sure he would free Israel, at the head of his host."

As he spoke, a flame sprang up between the piled logs in the forge. He went and picked up the tongs and the plowshare, now cold.

"The man I met seemed cheerful," he went on, laying the blade on the embers. "We talked about Jesus of Nazareth and his crucifixion, and he said a strange thing. I was so struck by it, I remember his words: 'Christ had to suffer like that in order to enter His glory.' I didn't know what that meant. It was getting dark, and he was alone and looked poor, so we invited him to eat with us. At the beginning of the meal, we noticed his hands. There was a hole through the middle of each palm."

"Were they torn?" asked Lazarus.

"No, pierced, as if by nails."

"He wasn't bleeding?"

"The wounds were raw, but they didn't bleed. . . . Who knows, maybe he inflicted them on himself."

Cleopas turned the share over. It was getting red-hot again.

"He behaved oddly at the table. He broke our loaf into pieces and passed them around, saying it was his body. When we asked him what he meant, he grew angry and told us we were blind. He said that, as the prophets foretold, he had risen from the dead on the third day. . . . Then we knew who he was."

He took the glowing metal and laid it flat on the anvil again.

"And you believed he was the Galilean come back from the dead?" asked Lazarus.

"When he was there in front of me, I did. Now, I'm not sure. . . ." He looked at Lazarus. "And I don't understand why the Galilean should have brought you back, just to leave you like that. . . ." He picked up his hammer. "Let me get on with my work. This messiah business has upset me. It doesn't make sense, and I don't want to talk about it any-more."

"And your brother? He saw him, too. Perhaps I could speak to him. . . ."

"He lives in Capernaum, and he's back there now. He came here only to spend Passover with me." Cleopas lifted his hammer and brought it down heavily.

"But what was he like?" Lazarus insisted, shouting to make himself heard over the noise. "Was he like me, with cracked, gray skin and the smell of rotting earth?"

"Had he been like you, I wouldn't have invited him into my house to share my bread. He was normal. Except for the wounds in his hands and in his feet, he was perfectly normal."

"Was there a wound in the chest, like a sword thrust?"

"I don't know," said Cleopas impatiently. "I didn't see one."

"Where was he headed?"

"Back to Galilee. He mentioned Tabgha. That's all I know."

Cleopas raised his hammer higher; the noise became deaf-ening. Seeing that the blacksmith meant to make further conversation impossible, and that nothing more would be got out of him, Lazarus reluctantly continued on his way.

He spent the night on a hill overlooking Emmaus. The interview with Cleopas had been vague, disappointing. All Lazarus learned was that the Nazarene had set out for Galilee. But should he believe the blacksmith, believe the appearance of the Galilean three days after his death? Why would the blacksmith invent such a story? To acquire importance in the eyes of the other villagers? No, Cleopas was obviously a simple, straightforward man incapable of such cunning. He admitted, even, that he might have been tricked.

But certain details did not fit. The holes in the hands, for example. Lazarus had seen the nails tear the victim's skin and flesh from the fingers and the palms. He had only to shut his eyes to see again that dreadful image. To see again the naked body in the rain, limp against the ropes beneath its arms. The soldier pulling at the ankles, until they came apart in tatters around the nails, which remained fixed in the wood of the cross. The broken body, when the ropes were released, falling into the mud. . . . Lazarus could forget nothing of it.

And what about the sword thrust in the Galilean's side? The blade had gone deep into the flesh, and a thin stream of blood, pale as water, had flowed out. . . . But perhaps Cleopas had not been able to see this wound because of the Galilean's tunic.

In any case, Lazarus could not imagine someone returning from the dead with a perfectly healthy complexion, and eating, drinking, walking with no difficulty. Miracle or no miracle, he could not imagine that. Had the Galilean not been shut up in the tomb for three days? And been tortured and maimed? How could he emerge from the Great Sleep with his body whole and his strength restored?

Lazarus debated whether he should embark on the long journey to the heart of Galilee, to Tabgha, on the distant shores of the Lake of Gennesaret. The heat of the day and the ravages of the sun did not deter him: he would travel at night. Nor did he fear bandits. If one smashed his head in with a rock, he would at least cease to see and hear and be aware of his own suffering. Why did he hesitate, then?

It was the thought of going so far away from Bethany, from Susannah and his sisters, and venturing into unknown territory. He dreaded being seen in towns and villages, exposed to people's mockery or disgust. And, although he desired to learn the truth, after his meeting with Cleopas he was afraid of what the truth might be. The truth, far from setting him free, might imprison him forever in absurdity and despair.

But when he remembered the interminable days he had spent behind the curtain in the upper room, and Susannah's frightened expression at night, his inclination to return home vanished completely.

It took him eleven days to reach the Lake of Gennesaret.

He avoided people and escaped the glare of the sun by starting each day's march at sunset. Steering clear of the barren heights of Jebel Qarantal, he went along the borders of Judea, through a monotonous arid waste far from trade and caravan routes. His eyes could scarcely see the stars, so he was able to get his bearings only when the sun rose. He followed the deposits of red silt between the hills. In the undifferentiating dimness of his sight, the hills appeared as slightly darker patches, which he imagined to be covered with terraced fields. At night he went slowly through the empty darkness, then the first gleams of dawn showed him whether or not he had gone astray. He would stop at the first clump of trees and spend the day resting in the shade. As the light and heat increased, he covered his face with his cloak and waited for the hours to pass. It was like being frozen in an eternity of his own. He tried but could not pray.

After two nights' march, his sandals, made of palm bark, were in shreds. He could not feel the cuts on his feet, but noticed that his pace was slower. So, despite his desire to avoid people, he left his lonely route and went into the nearest village. There, with a few coins he had got from Eliphas just before he set out, he bought a pair of Roman shoes. They were made of leather and had four thongs, which he fastened tightly to give support to his weak ankles.

As soon as he made out Mount Garizim in the distance, he changed direction and made for Jaffa and the sea, even though this meant a long detour and two or three more nights of walking. He did not want to go through Samaria, a country of outcasts whose priests were rebels and who worshiped Yahweh in their own sanctuary instead of going to pray in the Temple in Jerusalem. Lazarus, certain that God would not forgive him for setting foot on that impious soil, went instead through the wheat fields, pastures, and orchards of Sharon. Perhaps God would reward him for this.

At last, when he had lost count of how many nights it had been since he left Emmaus, he reached Galilee, and the unavoidable slopes of Mount Carmel. There, his half-forgotten dread of the revelations to come revisted him, as did his difficulty breathing. He had to rest every hundred paces. His ankles, too, began to fail him more often.

Yet, despite both weariness and fear, he continued on his way.

It was daybreak when he reached the shores of Lake Gennesaret. The first rays of the rising run struck coppery glints from the surface of the water. He could see the fishing boats as they came in to land their catch. He sat, exhausted, and though grayness veiled his sight, gazed at the landscape, at the ring of rounded hills still wreathed in darkness.

As the sky lightened, he saw little white towns around the lake, and he wondered which of the ports was Tabgha. A pale rosy glow spread over the hills, and the regular pattern of fields appeared on the gentle slopes. The water seemed to turn green, with mysterious long streaks of darker browns.

More than ten boats now approached the nearest group of houses, less than two hundred paces from where he sat. He watched. Men were moving about, some folding nets, others packing gleaming fish into large woven baskets. The captain shouted an order, and a young man, bare to the waist, jumped into water up to his shoulders, caught hold of a rope tied to the prow, and dragged the sturdy papyrus vessel to the shore. Lazarus averted his eyes. It was painful to watch other men at work.

When it was full daylight, he stood up, though he was still weak and his legs were shaky. He did not know how far it was to Tabgha, but if he delayed too long, he might not have the heart to go on. He resumed his journey.

It took him another night to reach Tabgha, on the far side of the lake. As soon as he got there, he questioned the village potter about the Galilean. The porter would say nothing. Then Lazarus asked the carpenter, the barber, and the sandal-maker. They all pretended to be too busy to answer.

He felt, that morning, that he could no longer bear the disgust and repugnance in people's faces. He would rather inspire fear than revulsion. But people did not fear him until they learned who and what he was. Should he tell everyone, then, that he was back from the dead? He had done nothing wrong, to be so despised. Would people ever stop treating him as a monstrous cripple, a degenerate being? Would they treat him thus in five hundred, in a thousand years?

About the third hour, immured in silence, wanting only to hide somewhere, and without the heart to approach any more of the villagers, Lazarus decided there was no point in standing there dumb and irresolute. If he avoided people's reactions, the faces they made, how would he ever find out the truth? He might as well go back to Bethany and lie down forever behind his curtain. . . . This thought was so appalling, it spurred him to question a fisherman, who was selling the last of his catch in the harbor. To Lazarus's surprise, the man answered, telling him about a "miraculous draft of fish" that had occurred one morning thanks to the very Jesus of Nazareth he was looking for.

"If you want to know more about it," said the man, "go and see Simon, son of Zacharias. He'll be delighted to tell you how, after spending the whole night without catching a single fish, at daybreak he hauled in a hundred and fifty-three big ones."

Lazarus's first impulse was to go and knock at Simon's door right away. But no, the man must be resting after his night's work; he wouldn't be very pleased to be disturbed. So Lazarus sat on the hill overlooking the village and there waited until nightfall.

When he saw the fishermen putting their nets on board their boats, he went back to the shore of the lake and asked to be directed to Simon, son of Zacharias.

Simon, who was lighting the oil lamps on his boat, showed no repugnance when Lazarus told him his name. "So it was you!" he said, looking Lazarus full in the face. "We've heard about you here, but I never thought I'd meet you."

"Tell me, please, what happened that morning of the miraculous draft of fish," said Lazarus. "Did you truly see the Galilean?"

"It's you who should be telling me what happened to you!" answered Simon. He paused, eyes shining. "I can't believe you're really standing in front of me!"

Lazarus, sensing that the man wanted to touch him, involuntarily drew back.

"Come," said Simon, taking his arm, "I must show you to the others!"

"No, wait, please! I don't want to see anyone else. Just tell me what happened, how you hauled in a hundred and fifty-three fish. I came here from Jerusalem. . . ."

Simon let go of his arm but kept staring at him.

Lazarus bowed his head. Even though the other's expression was anything but hostile, he couldn't bear being looked at like that.

"Are you hungry?" Simon asked. "Would you like some bread?"

"No, thank you," answered Lazarus. "I'm never hungry."

There was silence. Then someone called from another boat. The nets were on board, the lamps were lighted, and it was time to hoist the sails and leave.

"Listen," Simon said, "I can't talk to you now. Can you wait until morning? Or come with me in my boat, and we can talk while the nets are cast."

Lazarus glanced at the boat. There were three men aboard. He did not have the courage to spend the whole night in their company. "Just tell me in a few words what happened, please," he said. "I promise I'll wait here until you come back, and answer all your questions."

Lazarus entered the house, shut the door behind him. He stood in total darkness. Amazing, that Simon had given him the key to his home, letting him spend the night there in a real bed. No one had treated him like that, with kindness and concern, since he had returned from the grave. Admittedly, Simon wanted to be sure of finding Lazarus there in the morning, to hear from his own lips of his resurrection.

Groping his way, he found a bed in the middle of the room, and at once dropped his staff and cloak to the floor, took off his shoes, and lay down. For the first time in many days he had a roof over his head, was out of the cold and the damp.

As he lay on his back, exhausted, he went over in his mind the brief account Simon had given him before getting on the boat. After hours spent without catching anything, Simon and his companions were returning to shore, when a stranger came toward them, in the water, and told them to cast their net once again, to the right of the boat and farther out. Without knowing why, Simon helped the stranger into the boat and followed his instructions. Then, though there was no breath of wind, the water began to stir, and when the fishermen drew in their net, it contained a hundred and fifty-three large fish.

What did it matter, for the moment, if the story contained no proof? Simon had not noticed wounds on the Galilean's hands, but the whole thing had happened before it was really light. . . . When asked who he was, the stranger had answered, "I am a friend of James and of Peter, brother of Andrew, two fishermen you must have known here on the lake." And, indeed, Simon did remember a certain Peter, a huge fellow with tremendous strength. The big man with the goatee, probably.

Unfortunately, as soon as they reached the port, the stranger left them, refusing the fish they offered him by way of thanks. In the days that followed, Simon made inquiries among the people of Magdala and Capernaum. Several mentioned a miracle that had been performed on the other side of the lake some years earlier by a Galilean named Jesus, son of Joseph. He had multiplied a few loaves and fish to feed a whole crowd of hungry people who had come to listen to him. It was only then that Simon connected the stranger with the man who had been crucified in Jerusalem on the eve of Passover, and who was said by some to have risen from the dead.

Lazarus, lying motionless in the bed, puzzled over all this. Then, resolving to question Simon again in the morning, he let his mind empty.

Soon his legs grew as heavy as oak beams, and he felt a torpor creeping up from his ankles to his knees, to his stomach, shoulders, the back of his neck. For a moment he thought he was falling asleep, but, alas, he knew that that was impossible. He was too familiar with the pseudo-sleep into which he sometimes sank. He closed his eyes and let his thoughts unfold in a strangely slow procession. Several times he saw Susannah's face. She had colored ribbons in her hair, rouged cheeks, and her eyebrows lined and lengthened with bright blue. She came close, so close that her face almost touched his. And she smiled. She was no longer afraid.

A high-pitched shout from the village made him start, made him tremble. He seemed to be falling endlessly through space. He opened his eyes as wide as he could, but there was nothing around him but terrifying, impenetrable darkness.

Then, a burst of light. "There he is!" someone said. "The fool has gone to sleep!" People fell on him, hands seized him, just as they had on the day he came forth from the tomb. He fell heavily to the floor.

"What are you doing here?" someone bawled in his ear. "We'll teach you a lesson!"

In the faint light of a single oil lamp he saw a huge man with red hair, who reminded him of the giant with the goatee. I'm dreaming, he thought. I fell asleep at last, and I'm dreaming.

But someone hit him on the back with a stick—he was surrounded. Could one feel a blow so distinctly in a dream? Then he was shoved, and hit his forehead on a piece of furniture. "We'll teach you!" someone else laughed.

Lazarus, afraid, got up and tried to reach the door, but a foot tripped him. He fell on a pile of folded nets. The redhead grabbed him by the scruff of the neck. "Give back what you took!" he shouted, shaking him.

Lazarus realized he must have been seen entering Simon's house and taken for a thief. A wild thought occurred to him: to let them do what they liked with him—stone him, probably. With his head broken, he would not be able to think and worry anymore. He must seize the opportunity, and not try to defend himself, not tell them the truth.

The man with red hair lifted him up, held him in the air for a moment, then smacked him across the face, making him see stars.

"Where did you hide it?"

Many hands clawed at him. Despite his terror, Lazarus forced himself not to speak. More blows and insults rained down. He was spat on. Then they brought torches for light,

100

and the man with red hair, seeing Lazarus's face for the first time, released him.

"What's this?" he said with disgust. "Do any of you know this abortion?"

There was a murmur of bewilderment. No one knew him.

Lazarus started to crawl away. A man caught him by the ankle, but immediately let go. "He's like ice!"

Lazarus got to his feet, trembling. A few steps away was the gray rectangle of the open door. He could feel the night air. . . . But no, he must not run away. There might never be another chance like this to end it all. The man with red hair was standing in the way, brandishing an iron bar. "I'm not a thief," said Lazarus faintly. "I came from Jerusalem, to talk to Simon about the miraculous draft of fish. He knows I'm here. I've taken nothing. I'm ill. Let me go."

The huge figure stepped aside. Lazarus went through the door, but again was tripped, and fell on the stones of the courtyard. There was a roar of laughter behind him.

"Go, before I change my mind," shouted the man with red hair. "And don't come back!"

Lazarus dusted himself off. Where were his shoes, his staff, his cloak? He turned to go back for them, but the mocking, hostile rabble barred his way.

Barefoot, and ashamed of his cowardice, Lazarus limped off into the darkness.

Next morning, when light filtered into the cave where he had taken refuge, Lazarus was still beset by violent images: hand grabbing at his ankles, a big carroty head approaching, nearly touching him, behind it twenty jeering faces, and a fist cutting the gray gloom and sending a shower of stars before his eyes. Mustering all his strength, he tried to sweep these visions away with his hand. The rectangle of the door, his escape, still stood open to the night, but it was inaccessibly distant. . . .

I was asleep, he thought. All that was just a nightmare. I must shake it off. None of it happened.

But the figures that surrounded him, laughing, refused to go away; the man with red hair still pointed menacingly at him. "Give back what you took!" he shouted. Another blow, and the stars were replaced by a stony sun of dazzling white.

He tried to sit up. It had been no dream: there were big bruises on his arms, and although he really felt no pain, he did feel twinges in his face and all over his legs, and his back was stiff and sore.

More and more, he was losing his sense of reality.

He dragged himself to the mouth of the cave. Below, at the foot of the hill, he could see Tabgha. The fishermen had almost finished unloading their boats and packing their catch into big wicker baskets. Simon must be looking for him. Lazarus remembered his friendliness. What would Simon think when he heard what had happened at his house last night?

He ought to go down right away, but then he saw, again, the hostile mob outside Simon's house, holding torches and armed with sticks and iron bars. "Never set foot here again!" shouted the man with red hair.

Where was he to go now? He no longer wanted to learn the truth. People would not let him find it, with their silence, scorn, disgust. And if he persisted, what had happened last night would happen again.

But how was he going to find the strength to return to

Jerusalem, to repeat that interminable journey in the other direction? He had no shoes now, and no cloak to protect him from the cold. He fingered his tattered feet: would he be able to walk all that way? And for what? What awaited him in Bethany? Lying alone in the upper room behind the curtain, being spied on by his sisters? Seeing the fear on Susannah's face become more obvious each night?

He struggled all morning to drive away the images that plagued him. If he relaxed for a moment, the mob would reappear, led by the man with red hair. "He's there, in that cave!" they cried, swarming up the hill, armed with clubs. "That's where he's living now, hiding. He's in rags, barefoot, he lies there for hours without moving, staring into space. He can't defend himself, he can't escape!"

Lazarus could not understand their hatred. And I ran away, not because, if I were stoned to death, I'd never be able to find out the truth, he thought with shame. No—I ran because I was afraid of being beaten—even though I feel no pain now if someone hits me. . . . In the old days, I'd have stood my ground!

The only solution was to stay in this cave forever—alone, out of the sun and rain, far from other human beings and their stares, silence, hatred.

When darkness fell, he saw the little lights of the fishing boats moving out on the lake. He thought again of Simon. He, at least, had not rejected him.

Then he went back into the depths of the cave. His neck felt numb. As he was about to lie down on the hard ground, he rubbed it, and discovered that the cloth he had wrapped around it, to hide the gash, had been torn off in the attack on him here in Tabgha. He touched the wound; it was still dry, open, unhealed. He tore a strip off his tunic and tied that around his neck.

For two days and nights Lazarus lay in the cave, vainly trying to recapture the pseudo sleep he had experienced on Simon's bed. He stared for hours at the blackness above him.

The man with red hair and his rabble still pursued him with their torches, sticks, and iron bars. Lazarus could not shake off their image, or that of the torn and bloody hands.

He reflected that, even with his skull crushed in, lying at the bottom of the pit where criminals were stoned, he would still find himself suspended short of real death. Because he was doomed never to die. He would continue to exist, imprisoned in a broken body, unable to move or think properly, and his consciousness, already dimmed, would sink into another kind of horror, one impossible to imagine but certainly worse than anything that had gone before.

So he must give up considering *that* as a way out.

One thing, at least, was clear: he must not remain in the cave, tormented by those nightmare visions.

On the morning of the third day, Lazarus ventured out. Once again he saw the lake below, the fishermen unloading their catch and spreading their nets out to dry. The rolling hills were reflected in the still water. A scene so peaceful, it seemed to exist out of time. . . .

He must go to Jerusalem and look for the big man with the goatee and the fair young man named John. Why had he not done that to begin with? They were bound to know something. But, even if he found where they were hiding, would they speak to him, tell him whether or not they had stolen the

Galilean's body from the tomb? Also, if the Galilean really had risen from the dead, he must, at some time or other, have gone to his home in Nazareth, to see his father and mother and childhood friends. His parents, although they might not have been able to make him stay with them, would surely know where he could be found.

Lazarus decided to go to Nazareth first.

When it began to grow dark, he pulled two strips of bark from a dead tree. These, twisted with strips of cloth torn from the hem of his tunic for strength, he tied to the soles of his feet. He found a stick to replace the staff he had lost. Then, more to escape his emptiness and fear than to seek a truth he no longer really hoped to find, he set out once more.

When he reached Nazareth, Lazarus had no trouble picking out the carpenter's house from among the simple white semi-cubical dwellings huddled at the base of the limestone cliff behind them. He looked in through the window of the workshop, a square hole in a rough mud wall, and saw an empty bench covered with dust. An ax with a cracked handle lay in a corner with rusty knives and saw blades. A heap of crooked nails, a hammer, and a broken try square were strewn near a half-open door. A table with only two legs stood upside down and unfinished on the other side of the room. There was no sign of sawdust on the mud floor; not a single plank, not a single log, waited against the wall to be cut or trimmed.

An abandoned workshop. Moving away, he surveyed the house. It, too, looked empty. Had his journey been for nothing?

When he went up and pushed the door, it opened.

He found himself in a dark hallway that ended in a flight of stairs leading down. A curtain hung at the bottom of the stairway. It was the first time Lazarus had been in this kind of house, not uncommon in Galilee. The narrow hall, with its ceiling suddenly sloping down to where the house itself was hollowed out of the rock, reminded him irresistibly of the entrance to his tomb.

At the foot of the stairs, Lazarus stopped and listened. All he could hear was his own breathing, shallow and hoarse. Gently pushing aside the curtain, he entered a bare room poorly lighted: a few sunbeams filtered through small holes in the curved roof. A woman with long gray hair had her back to him. Seated on a mat near a bed cut out of the rock like a ledge in a funeral chamber, she was twisting, pressing, and rolling threads of linen onto a spindle. When she turned toward him, he recognized her. The last time he had seen her, she was dressed in black and drenched with rain at the foot of the cross. Holding in her arms the bloody naked body of the Galilean.

She did not stare at him now, as everyone else did. Nor did she seem surprised to see him there. She did not ask him what he wanted. It was as if she recognized him, too, and guessed why he had come.

He was the first to speak. "Are you the mother of the man who was crucified in Jerusalem on the eve of Passover?" he asked.

"Yes," she answered softly, wearily.

"I've been told that he rose from the dead. . . . I'm Lazarus, the man he brought back from the grave in Bethany. Did he really come back to life? Do you know where he is? I've been looking for him for a long time!"

She wound a few more linen fibers around the wooden spindle. Lazarus noticed the prominent blue, almost black, veins under the wrinkled skin of her hands. "I am certain he is risen from the dead," she said, getting up. "Many people have seen him, and he was definitely alive." She put the spindle down on a chest and went and sat on a bench. Her movements were slow and careful, like those of an old woman.

"But when they saw him, was he 'alive' in the same way I am?" asked Lazarus.

She looked at him calmly. She was under three rays of light coming in through the ceiling. Strangely, despite her gray hair and the innumerable wrinkles around her slightly sunken mouth, there was something about her, about her face, that made her seem young. It occurred to him that she must have been beautiful once.

"Peter, Thomas, and John saw him," she said, "and they recognized him at once. They shared their bread with him. He was very different from you."

"He didn't bear the marks of death on his body, as I do?"

"He still had the wounds in his hands and feet and the mark of the sword in his side. I know, because Thomas would not believe he was risen from the dead and put his hand into all the wounds. . . ." She looked away. "That's all I can tell you. I stayed in Jerusalem for thirty days in the hope of seeing him, but I never did. Then I fell ill and returned to Nazareth. If he's coming to see me, he's as likely to come here as anywhere else—this is his home. I'm not worried: he will do what has to be done in his own good time."

"But why isn't he like me, after spending three days in the grave? You can see what it did to me."

She looked at him again, but there was no sign of compassion in her face. "I can't say. But fear not—everything he does is for the glory of God. If he brought you back to life, he had good reasons for it. You simply cannot understand the meaning of what he did for you. Do you think even I, his mother, always understood what he did? Do you think I understand why he went out of his way to get himself crucified? Why he, who could be violent, did nothing to stop them from nailing him to the cross?"

"I, too, was at Golgotha when he died," said Lazarus. "I saw you take up his body covered with mud. I still hear your cries inside my head. . . . For me, he was the Messiah, and I had hoped he would perform another miracle, one that would truly restore me to life. . . . The Messiah should not die like a thief."

"And what would you have done with your new life, had he removed all the marks of death from your body?"

"I would have gone back to my work, and would have borne witness for him. I would not have let them crucify him. . . . Perhaps I would have followed him, like John and Peter."

"He has enough followers, and probably would not have wanted you to join him. He expects something else from you."

"What? What does he want from me?"

"I don't know. Only he can say."

They were silent for a while. The Galilean's mother sat motionless on her stone bench.

"He would have done better to leave me in my tomb," said Lazarus quietly. "Why did he come? I never asked him to!"

"You must not think that your suffering does not touch me," said the woman with a gentle smile. "I feel for you. But I do not pity you. No, I envy you. It is a wonderful thing that has happened to you. I only hope you realize it one day."

"You haven't answered my questions," Lazarus said, not understanding. "I should not have come."

She gazed at him, as if weighing him, as one looked upon a child—impartially, without tenderness or indulgence. He suddenly wanted to leave.

"I must see him!" he cried. "Do you think he'll come to see you? I'm so tired of searching."

"I will die soon myself," she answered softly. "He has been risen from the dead sixty days now, and he knows I cannot wait much longer. If he is really still among us—and I do not know whether he is or not—and if he means to come and see me, it will have to be soon. If you want to stay here and wait with me, you can—I don't mind. But I cannot promise you he'll come. . . ."

She looked at his feet, at the worn pieces of bark. "But if you prefer to return to Jerusalem and talk to Peter and Thomas, who saw him, and to John, the best of his disciples, take the sandals and cloak that are in the room behind the workshop. They belonged to Joseph, my husband. You will need them on your journey."

As soon as he left the city, by the Ephraim Gate, Jair could see the seven crosses on Golgotha. He could see Esau, nails through his hands and feet, his body sagging, his legs limp and bent.

So they had not lied to him: blood was being shed again in Jerusalem. His heart started to pound: perhaps Esau was already dead.

Ignoring the armed guards, he made his way toward the Hill of the Skull.

It was outrageous of Pilate to help himself to the treasures of the Temple, even though he claimed he had done it to raise the money for two new aqueducts to bring spring water to the city. The Romans made enough money from their taxes; they did not need to steal to finance their public works. On the other hand, was opposing them worth the cost of one's own life? What was the point of rebelling, if it always ended the same way? True, the year before, Pilate had finally given in to public opinion and taken down the hundreds of flags bearing portraits of Caesar that he had had put up all over the city, even in the courtyard of the Temple. Was it likely, though, that he would give up this latest idea of cutting the upper city in two with aqueducts?

Even if Pilate did back down, were all these fresh sacrifices worth it?

No one else was there to bear the dying men company. Jair went over to the crosses and looked up at Esau. Esau was still a boy. His head hung down on his chest, his hair covering his smooth young face. The crossbeam was stained with blood from his hands. The almost imperceptible rise and fall of his chest showed that he was still breathing.

Jair, in distress, thought of the hours Esau had spent with him at the Pool of Siloam just before Passover; of how Esau had made him tell the story, over and over again, of how he was cured; of how Esau had pressed him to say whether he thought the Messiah, the warrior who would save Israel, had come at last.

Black birds were already wheeling in the sky above the crosses. Soon their beaks would tear at that still-warm flesh.

"What are you doing?" yelled a soldier in the almost incomprehensible mixture of Greek and Aramaic most Romans used to address Jews. "Don't you know no one's allowed here?" He went up to Jair, spear at the ready.

Jair held out his arms to show that he had no weapon.

"You want to end up like that?" asked the legionary, applying the tip of his spear to Jair's stomach and jerking his head toward the men on the crosses. "Know any of them?"

"No," lied Jair. "I came out of curiosity."

"Well, if you're so curious, have a good look! They took up arms against Rome, and what's happened to them will happen to you, if you follow their example! Now go, and count yourself lucky I didn't arrest you!"

Jair turned back toward the Ephraim Gate. There was no point in taking unnecessary risks. He made his way to the lower city. Many of the shops were closed in protest against the cruelty of the Romans, and the streets, usually so noisy and full of people, were empty. But odors of fried garlic, oil, and freshly baked bread wafting from the houses showed that life still went on within the shelter of walls and courtyards.

Going by an open door, he heard laughter, and then Keturah's voice calling him. "Jair! Jair! Come in and have a drink!"

A fat woman rushed out, seized him by the arm, and dragged him inside. Her hand was damp, her dress stained, and she smelled of wine. Having just seen Esau, Jair didn't feel like offering resistance. He was greeted with cries and exclamations and made to sit at a table. A cup of wine was thrust into his hands. For a few moments, before his eyes grew accustomed to the dimmer light, he was blind again. Then the faces of Javan and Asshur slowly took shape. Two women he did not know were hanging on them, fondling them. Disgusted, Jair pushed the wine aside. "I'm not thirsty," he said.

"You're gloomy today, Jair!" said Keturah in her strident voice. "What's the matter?" She put her massive arm around his neck and snuggled up to him.

"Don't waste your time," he said. "I'm out of money."

112

"That's all right, dear," she said. "For once, you can have me as a gift." She pressed her wet lips to his cheek, then took his hand and guided it to her naked breast. Feeling the sweat on her skin, he tried to draw away, but she would not let him go.

One of the women on the other side of the table put her mouth to Javan's and spit wine into it. Javan, taken by surprise, grunted, and the wine spilled out over his chin and tunic. Keturah roared with laughter and told Jair to do the same to her.

"No," he said. "I don't feel like playing today."

"What's wrong?' she whined. "I told you you could have me free tonight."

"I just saw Esau on Golgotha," he answered simply.

"I always said you would have been better off staying blind!" Asshur laughed. "That way, you wouldn't have seen anyone crucified, and you'd have gone on thinking Keturah was young and pretty!"

"So why don't you take up arms against the Romans?" said Javan.

Jair shrugged and turned away. They went on making fun of him, but he stopped listening. All he could think of was the boy on the cross.

After a while he noticed that Keturah had slipped her hand under his tunic and was stroking the hair on his chest. Without thinking, he picked up the cup in front of him and put it to his lips. The wine was sour. He could feel Keturah's hot breath full in his face. When her fat fingers moved down toward his stomach, he pushed her away, more firmly this time.

"You're strange today!" she bawled. "If you don't want me anymore, just say so!"

He replied that he was tired; that he thought he had better go back and spend the night by the Pool of Siloam.

Javan stood up. "You're right!" he said. "It's time for bed." Off he went with the woman who had been clinging to him. But before he disappeared behind the curtain at the back of the room, he turned. "By the way, Jair, someone was asking about you today. A strange character, not normal, with a gray face. He stank. He wanted to see you."

"Why?"

"I don't know. We threw him out, he smelled so awful." Then he added: "He probably thinks you can perform miracles, too!"

Jair awoke in the middle of the night. Keturah was asleep on the blanket beside him, breathing noisily, her mouth open. She reeked of sweat and wine. He drew his cloak up over her large bosom, in order not to see it. The night was hot, and the stars dotting the sky above the flat roof where they lay merged into a milky haze. He could still see Esau nailed to the cross. . . .

Was it because Esau feared that the warrior messiah would never come that he had finally joined the Zealots and taken up arms? Jair remembered trying to explain to him by the Pool of Siloam why killing all the Romans would be no solution. He recalled seeing him again a few days ago in the streets of Jerusalem. Esau had pretended not to know him. The hatred in his eyes was like the point of a sword.

Jair, in a way, felt responsible for what had happened. Admittedly he was not educated and did not understand everything; indeed, many things were completely beyond him. But that was no excuse.

Jair was one of those who blamed themselves for sins they did not commit.

Lazarus had been back in Jerusalem for several days, wandering the streets from morning till night in the hope of finding John or the big man with the goatee. But neither had been seen.

He would have preferred to hide in some dark corner and stay there forever, but forced himself to go where the crowds were thickest, to the two markets, which were closed only at night and on the Sabbath. First, the market in the upper city, which was well stocked and elegant, with stalls selling jewelry, silks, embroidered shirts, leather shoes, bright-colored carpets, gold plate, and perfume. Lazarus went slowly, scrutinizing every merchant, every customer, every passer-by, and especially the many beggars who, attracted by the wealth of the rich, flocked to these streets and alleys.

Then, the noisy market in the lower city, where villagers from the surrounding countryside sold grain, figs, wine, tools, thick camel's-hair cloaks, fish, donkeys, and sheep. Women from Judea sold fine woolen goods; those from Samaria, garments made of linen. Lazarus merged with the crowd, protected by the noise and bustle. People were too busy to notice him. Sometimes he forgot what he was there for, and wandered aimlessly, paying no attention to the pushing and shoving, the agitation around him.

Or he simply walked in the city. When he tired, he sat in some dark alley and stared into space.

Why did he stay in Jerusalem? No one mentioned the Galilean now; it was as if the Galilean had been forgotten. What was the point, then, of wandering all day like the derelicts and loafers who did nothing but stretch out their hands for alms and wait for time to pass? He thought about how industrious he had been in earlier days, how he had delighted in his work, and the rich, full life that had once been his.

Now he was incapable of anything, useless. He did not even have the strength to rebel against the unjust God who had inflicted this horror upon him.

Sometimes he thought of his journey through Judea, Samaria, and Galilee, and how it had led to nothing but the terrible night when the man with red hair and the people of Tabgha had driven him away like a thief. And even Simon's story no longer offered hope. On Lake Gennesaret, everyone knew that sudden squalls could suddenly make shoals of fish appear in unlikely places.

As for the visit to the Galilean's mother in Nazareth, all Lazarus could remember was the cold tranquillity on the face of the old woman, who had no knowledge of her son or of what had happened after he was laid in his tomb.

When the trumpets announcing the end of the day sounded over the city, Lazarus would leave Jerusalem and set out for the Hill of Evil Counsel, beyond Gehenna. He walked through the pestilential vapors of the city's sewage, past burning heaps of animal carcasses and other noisome garbage. It was not unusual for ragged figures to emerge from the gray haze to watch him pass, leaning on his staff. Armed like bandits, almost naked, and black with grease and soot, they stared at the strange being that was more grotesque than they were,

116

as he vanished in the fading light in the direction of the hills.

He would spend the night beneath an olive tree. One by one the lights in the city were extinguished, and when the last gleams, like distant stars, went out behind the walls, all he could see below was a vast emptiness devoid of color, shape, or life.

On the morning of the second Sabbath after his return, when he was wandering near the canal in the Sion district, he overheard a strange conversation in a deserted alley.

Four men were sitting on a narrow flight of steps between two rows of houses. As Lazarus labored up the steps, he heard one of them mention a certain Naham, a cripple who had been cured by a miracle in Capernaum before Passover.

"He was found dead in a field with his throat cut," said the man.

"Why were they so afraid of him?" asked another.

Lazarus, intrigued, stopped to listen.

"They think we want to destroy them," said the oldest of the four.

At that point, one of them noticed Lazarus and whispered something to his companions, who immediately fell silent.

Seeing their suspicious looks, Lazarus supposed they took him for a spy and thought it best to continue his slow ascent to the upper city.

That evening he did not wait for the sound of the trumpets before going to sit under the olive tree. There, he gazed back at the city and thought about the four men and their whispered conversation.

Who was Naham, once cured by a miracle in Capernaum and now found slain in a field?

117

It occurred to Lazarus that the stranger who had stabbed him in Bethany may not have been a robber.

Beggars and cripples crowded around the Pool of Siloam, near the ancient city of David. Some took shelter under the tall porticos built by Herod the Great; others huddled below, around the muddy tank and the worn stone steps leading down to it.

Night and day, the place swarmed with the poor and the needy.

In the weeks after Jair's miraculous cure, the throng at the holy place grew even denser. Everyone wanted to touch the man, blind from birth, whose sight had been restored by a mixture of mud and saliva put on his eyelids. They came to hear the story from his own lips. For nearly a month, and no matter how often he told the hundreds of ailing people that he did not understand what had happened to him, and could do nothing for them, they jostled and fought to get near him.

He told them, over and over, to go and see *him*. "When he touched my eyes," he said, "I shouted at him to stop. But he kept pressing on my eyes, hurting me, while everyone laughed. And then a warmth slowly spread over my eyes, and I began to see. He's the one you want. The one with the power. If you believe in him, if you believe he really is the son of God, maybe he will help you."

But no matter what Jair said and no matter where he went, dozens of poor wretches followed him. He was an object of respect, envy, and curiosity. A member of the Sanhedrin, even, came to question him.

Then, a few days before Passover, came the news that the

Galilean had been arrested. All the commotion over Jair died away, and the Pool of Siloam went back to what it had been before—one of the many places where the poor of Jerusalem gathered.

People didn't look twice at Jair, and his extraordinary cure was forgotten. This pleased him, since he disliked being singled out, leading the same wretched existence as before and having done nothing to deserve special attention. He had even been unable to speak about the Galilean properly, as was proved by the fact that his attempts to explain things to Esau and calm him down in the Galilean's name had only led the boy to Golgotha.

That morning, wanting to keep well away from Keturah, Javan, and the rest, Jair sat begging, as he often did, under the columns at the top of the steps that led to the murky waters of the Pool of Siloam, when he saw a strange individual coming toward him. Bent and emaciated, the man leaned on a staff; his face was gray and bony.

Are the sick starting to come and ask about the miracle again, Jair wondered, surprised that this should happen after three months of silence.

The man halted less than three paces away. Never, among all the unfortunates Jair had seen since his sight was restored, had he looked upon such a face. Then he caught the smell coming from the man—earth and damp roots. This was no ordinary sufferer.

"I am Lazarus," the man said simply, in a toneless voice. "The man from Bethany who was brought back from the dead."

At first Jair thought he was lying. He knew, of course, about the carpenter. That had been shortly after his own sight

119

was restored. But he could not believe that Lazarus, whom everyone knew to be hiding away from human eyes, had emerged from his concealment just to visit him.

Then Jair remembered what Javan had said the day before, about a strange character looking for him. This man, truly, bore the signs of death, seemed the very incarnation of death. He had nothing in common with Jair, who had really been cured by a miracle. Born blind, Jair now could see the smallest star in the sky!

The stranger, not waiting for a reply, asked if Jair had seen the Galilean's friends again. He had been looking for them for weeks, he said. He wanted to talk to them.

He spoke slowly, in a monotone. Jair, feeling his icy breath, decided to leave—he did not like talking to this man. But Lazarus stared fixedly at him with leaden eyes—and suddenly seemed so pathetic, Jair felt that he should help him. The only friend of the Galilean's he had seen, he said, was John, one day in the Street of the Fullers, John, however, although he knew Jair well, having been there by the pool at the time of the miracle, had pretended not to see him.

"They believe they are in danger," said Jair, "and the troubles of the last few days, with soldiers all over Jerusalem, are not likely to bring them out of hiding. Ever since the Galilean was crucified, they have feared for their lives. But I think I know where they are. Sometimes people go to see them after dark. I never have."

"Could you show me the house?"

Jair hesitated. Was it really possible that this defective creature had been the subject of a miracle? Had Jair let himself be carried away by pity and said too much? Who knew whether the stranger's intentions were friendly or not? And what did he want with the Galilean's friends?

Thirty years of blindness had given Jair the ability to guess people's thoughts, desires, and ulterior motives from a sigh, the intonation of a voice, even the rustle of a garment. Yet he could not tell whether Lazarus was speaking the truth or concealing some evil purpose. He must be careful not to put the Galilean's friends in danger.

But the broken figure standing before him seemed the embodiment of despair. Should Jair trust his intuition? When the Galilean had first touched his eyes, he had taken it for an act of aggression, had shouted to him to stop.

In Judea, it was against etiquette to look people in the face too directly, yet the two continued to stare at each other. Lazarus was waiting for his question to be answered, but Jair was reluctant to reveal John's hiding place. He decided to test Lazarus first.

"You were in the realm of the dead?" he asked.

"Yes," said Lazarus.

"What . . . is it like?" Jair asked, almost in a whisper.

"Like nothing," was the answer.

"But what did you see when you were dead? Where did you go?"

"I saw nothing, went nowhere. Everyone asks what death is, but it isn't anything. It's darkness, silence. It doesn't exist."

Again Jair felt like running away.

"I was dead," said Lazarus, bowing his head. "But I did not suffer. Believe me, there is no death. Nor life, for me. Nothing exists anymore."

"Don't you believe in anything?" cried Jair, appalled by such despair. "Not even in him who brought you back to life?"

"No," said Lazarus. "I wish to God he had left me in my tomb."

Jair, who revered the memory of the Galilean, could not understand this.

The stranger sat down on the step beside him. Jair edged away from the cold that came from his body. The man's empty eyes wandered into the distance. He was in no hurry, and probably would wait indefinitely for an answer to his question.

Jair, saying nothing, started to beg again. He's only another derelict, he thought. No reason I should drive him away. The Pool of Siloam belongs to everybody. . . . But if I don't want to, I don't have to tell him where John and the others are hiding.

At noon, trying to forget the uneasiness the stranger caused in him, as well as his anger at the way the stranger had spoken about the Galilean, Jair drew the only piece of bread he had from his bag and held it out. Lazarus took it, considered it, then put it to his mouth.

"I don't usually eat at all now," he said, taking a small bite and handing it back.

Jair looked at the scarcely touched bread taken from those yellow fingers. His hand trembled. Fighting to overcome his revulsion, he took a bite himself. It tasted of earth and corpses, and he gulped it down almost without chewing. He offered the bread to Lazarus again, but Lazarus refused it.

Then Jair forced himself to eat it all, every crumb. At the time, he did not know why.

That night, Lazarus went to the place Jair had arranged for them to meet, the entrance to the Street of the Potters. The first to arrive, he waited. He was uneasy, not yet sure that Jair would take him to where John was hiding. Jair's attitude puzzled him. Like Lazarus, he had had a miracle happen to him, but he behaved differently. He seemed to want to help Lazarus, but was also afraid of him, and not only because of the marks of death on Lazarus's body.

After Jair had shared his bread with him—a clear gesture of good will, in contrast to his visible doubt and suspicion—they had talked. Lazarus told him of his fruitless search through Judea, Samaria, and Galilee. Jair listened carefully and asked many questions—about the blacksmith at Emmaus, about the miraculous draft of fish, and especially about the Galilean's mother. Jair frowned when Lazarus said she had been cold, but made no comment.

The two had sat there on the steps for more than an hour. Sometimes Lazarus felt that Jair believed what he was saying, that Jair was almost like a friend. Sometimes Jair seemed distant, incredulous, or even scandalized by the way Lazarus described his thoughts or the people he had encountered. Then finally, after long reflection, Jair, looking tense, agreed to meet him at nightfall.

Before they had parted, Lazarus asked about Naham, the former cripple found with his throat cut in Capernaum, but Jair knew nothing about that, and had not been attacked himself.

At last he appeared in the middle of the street. Lazarus went to him. "Follow me," said Jair.

123

They made their way between the stalls of the potters, who, on this Sabbath eve, were waiting to shut up their shops as soon as the first notes of the ram's horn sounded from the roof of the Temple, above the Holy of Holies. There were still many people in the street. A Roman officer and four legionaries, all armed, passed them. Lazarus, who had heard that two centurions had been murdered by the Zealots near Herod's Palace, was surprised to see soldiers venturing into this part of the lower city, where at any moment they might get a knife in the back. He had heard that there had been thirty arrests in the last few days, and that more crucifixions were imminent.

Keeping up with Jair, in order not to be separated from him in the crush in the narrow street, Lazarus could feel the other's eyes on him almost constantly. But the look was not one of scorn or disgust. It expressed, instead, puzzlement, doubt. Yet he was sure Jair was taking him to the house where John was.

Because of the crowd blocking the way, they were held up outside a large workshop. Two men turned wheels with their feet, while their hands carefully gave shape to the clay. Another sat nearby painting basins and bowls. A fourth stood at the counter in the front of the shop selling jars for grain, braziers, writing tablets, terra-cotta toys, little oil lamps, long-necked pitchers with handles, large cooking pots. . . .

Lazarus realized that he no longer minded seeing other men at work. This new indifference frightened him. Soon, perhaps, he would be resigned to his fate, and then there would be no more hope.

They turned into a dark, deserted alley between very old

houses. After thirty or so paces, Jair pointed to a small single-story house, roughly built of gray stone.

"There," he said. "No need for me to stay. They won't want to talk to me, I'm sure." He faced Lazarus. "I'm trusting you. I don't know if I'm doing the right thing. I don't know you. Much of what you say seems crazy. Who knows if it is the truth." He moved away. "May you find here what you seek," he said as he left.

Lazarus, wondering if he should wait for John or the big man with the goatee to come out, stood alone outside the closed-up house. The windows were covered by heavy curtains. The place seemed empty. Perhaps they had left Jerusalem after the recent trouble. . . . Better to find out now. Lazarus went to knock at the door, but hesitated.

What am I doing, he thought. If they tell me that yes, they stole the Galilean's body, or if I guess that they did from what they say or do, what remains for me to believe in or hope for? I'm almost certain that there has been no resurrection but mine. Why keep on searching for the truth, when the only refuge left to me is a faint doubt, and if I eliminate that doubt . . .

He looked back at the Street of the Potters and its lights. There, some sort of life still went on, with an element of uncertainty that was worth preserving at all costs.

He looked at the heavy, studded wooden door. He listened, heard nothing. Clenching his fist, raising his arm again, he knocked as hard as he could.

"Almighty God," he said—he who no longer prayed—"Almighty God . . . let them not be in."

That night, on the roof, Jair made love to Keturah with unusual ardor. He possessed her two times, in quick succession. Wanting more, she mounted him frenziedly, her flabby stomach pressed heavily against his flat one, and forced him to enter her again. Although he was both weary and revolted, he did not resist. He could see her big face swaying over him against the starry sky. A drop of sweat fell on the corner of his mouth. He shut his eyes. She was panting loudly. Her weight made it difficult for him to breathe. Why did he do this, when he had not the least desire?

She put her fingers in his hair and stroked his head. He touched her large hips, arched his back, and felt himself penetrating her more deeply than before, though it was as if he were on the rack. In a hoarse croak she begged him to go farther still. But by now it hurt. A hot thick tongue forced his lips apart. Her saliva tasted of wine; he swallowed it.

Before he had gone to meet Lazarus of Bethany, he had sworn he would not spend the night with her. But then, passing her house on the way to the Pool of Siloam, he could not stop himself from going in. It was because of Lazarus, the man back from the dead, that he was doing the opposite of what he wanted. He was sure of that.

At every jolt of Keturah's body he could smell her acrid sweat. He put his hands on her hot, clammy back, which was endlessly rocking. . . .

He remembered Lazarus's unfeeling words about the Galilean's mother, and Lazarus's skepticism about the power of the Galilean himself, who had brought him out of the Great Sleep. Lazarus even referred to him sometimes as "the magician." Had he never heard about the poor people on Mount Scopus and in the courtyard of the Temple? Did he not know that once the Galilean had risked his life to save a prostitute from stoning? Had taken, trembling, the rocks from the hands of those who wanted to carry out the Law? Was that the behavior of a mere maker of magic? . . . Jair was sorry, now, that he had taken him to John's house.

Keturah pinched his chest, then pressed her mouth to his again. Why did he seek pleasure with her like this, when it nearly always ended in disgust? He must stop it. But she was so heavy! Instead of trying to free himself, he returned her kiss.

He could not understand why everything he did was the opposite of what he intended. Why suddenly he began to move his body faster. Why he seized the woman by the hair and pulled her head back. A stifling wave of heat swept over him. He opened his eyes, and the sky, white with stars, careened above the huge dark face with its disheveled hair. He gripped Keturah's clammy neck; she let out a little cry. And painfully he put forth all his strength in an attempt to be through with her, at least for tonight.

Jair awoke as the first mauve streaks of dawn appeared in the sky over Jerusalem. Today was the Sabbath, and, though it was not yet light, he decided to go to the Temple to pray. As he was getting up, he found that he had soiled his tunic the night before, embracing Keturah while he was still dressed. He wrapped his cloak around him to hide the telltale spots and left without a backward glance at the bulky figure still asleep there on the roof.

It was so early, the streets were empty, and he soon reached the double gates leading to the Court of the Gentiles. His attention was attracted at once to the dozens of torches burning over the Royal Portico. As he drew nearer, he saw about fifty Roman soldiers assembled. Their coats of mail and iron helmets gleamed in the light of the torches. Each soldier held in one hand a broad, curved wooden shield; in the other, a sharp, heavy javelin. It was clear they were there to keep an eye on the Jews as the Jews prayed to their God.

Jair felt a twinge of anger. How long must these infidels be allowed to defile the land chosen by the Almighty? For a moment, it seemed to him that Esau had been right to rebel. Then he remembered how the Galilean had said that Rome's oppression of the children of Israel, compared to the falsehood and hypocrisy with which the Jews condemned themselves to darkness, was the lesser of two evils.

He entered the courtyard. Looking up, he saw that there were at least two hundred soldiers lined up along its perimeter, surveying the area below. Trying to ignore their presence, he made for the Gate Beautiful and went up the steps and into the Court of the Women. The Levites, accompanied by harp and tabor, horn and trumpet, were starting to chant the psalms of the day, sometimes in unison, sometimes in counterpoint. Farther in, beyond the bronze, gold, and silver Nicador Gate, which had just been thrown open, the priests were offering up sheep on the altar, the sacrifice lighted by ruddy flames from the great braziers.

Jair put his cloak over his head and went forward among the now numerous faithful. When he reached the Court of the Jews, he bowed and, so that God might help him stop acting like a madman, whose actions contradicted his intentions, there, surrounded by Jews reciting twice over the tra-

128

ditional Shema, he slowly repeated the prayer the Galilean once taught his followers:

> *Our father who art above us,*
> *reveal thyself as Lord.*
> *May thy kingdom come,*
> *and thy will be accomplished*
> *on earth as its image in heaven.*
> *Give us our daily bread, for we hunger,*
> *forgive us our wrongs against thee*
> *as we forgive those who have wronged us,*
> *and do not expose us to temptation,*
> *but deliver us from the Tempter.*

When Jair got back to the Pool of Siloam, he was surprised to find Lazarus there: he had not expected to see him again. Lazarus sat at the foot of the steps, watching a cripple who was hanging on to a column and dangling his useless legs in the muddy water.

Jair went straight to Lazarus and asked him what had happened.

"I didn't see John," said Lazarus, not looking at him. "Or the big man with the goatee. Or any of the rest of the Galilean's disciples. I kept knocking at the door and calling, and I'm sure they were there, because I heard a noise inside. I asked them to open up, I told them who I was and that I needed to talk to them, but they did not open the door. . . . I stayed there all night, but it was no use. . . . Now I'll never know the truth, never know why this happened to me, who did nothing to deserve it."

Again, Jair felt the impulse to help him.

Lazarus continued to stare at the skeletal legs the cripple was bathing in the dirty water. "You, the Galilean rescued from darkness. Me, for no reason at all, he plunged into the blackest possible night."

That evening, Lazarus went back to the dark, empty street between old rough stone houses and banged at John's door longer and louder than he had the night before. After his despair and resignation, a desire to *know* had returned, stronger than ever. He realized that since his meeting with Jair two days ago, he had changed: he felt an anger and rebelliousness much fiercer than what he had known before. His resentment against the Galilean was greater, now that he had met a man who had been the subject of a *real* miracle—Jair, born blind, could see the smallest star in the firmament.

Lazarus knocked until he was exhausted, then sat on the ground with his back to the wall. I'll wait all night, he thought. And if necessary, I'll come back tomorrow.

Soon the lights went out in the Street of the Potters, and he was alone in the half-dark of the sultry summer night. He looked up at the sky—for him, a flat expanse unrelieved by the gleam of any star.

He thought of Jair and his advice to persevere: sooner or later, he said, Lazarus would find what he was looking for. "John and the others won't have a thing to do with me, but with you I'm sure it will be different. They'll help you because you need their help. They'll take you to where the Galilean has been hiding since his resurrection."

Lazarus could not understand why Jair took an interest in

him, why he stayed with him till evening, asking questions, and leaving only now and then to go to the top of the steps and beg. But then hadn't Lazarus gone back at dawn to the Pool of Siloam just in the hope of seeing him?

Again Jair shared his bread with him. Did he guess, Lazarus wondered, that I only agreed to take a bite of bread, before, to see if he could bring himself to touch it afterward?

Lazarus dismissed Jair from his mind, tired of asking himself questions to which there were no answers. He shut his eyes and stretched out his legs. He waited, hoping that numbness would creep upward from his ankles to his stomach. . . . He tried to imagine himself swinging gently between the walls of a bottomless pit. But all he could see was the cripple bathing his lifeless legs in the muddy pool. The anger growing inside Lazarus prevented him from making his mind blank and sinking into the pseudo slumber that had once obliterated his blackest thoughts.

He found himself thinking that the Galilean's sufferings on the cross were no more than he deserved. Not only had the Galilean given Jair his sight, but he had also filled his heart with kindness and generosity, whereas the heart of Lazarus was eaten by anger and hate.

When he opened his eyes, he saw a dog looking at him from a small distance. He called it, and it came over slowly, put its cold, damp nose to his feet, and began to sniff. It wagged its tail, apparently neither disgusted nor afraid. Lazarus could see that the creature's coat was dull and mangy; that it was thin and had a half-healed sore on its side. The dog pushed its muzzle between his knees, its foraging limited by his tunic. Lazarus kept still, so as not to frighten it. When it looked up, Lazarus imagined sadness and friendliness in those yellow eyes. He stretched out his hand to stroke its ear gently. The dog let him do so for a few moments, then suddenly ran off.

Nothing else happened that night. Lazarus leaned against the wall as the useless hours went by. At daybreak he returned to the Pool of Siloam.

After another day spent with Jair, mostly in silence, he went back to John's house. But this time he did not knock at the door. Instead, he sat on the other side of the street, some distance away, in a recess. Perhaps it was a mistake to keep coming back like this. The Galilean's friends had probably left Jerusalem. But Lazarus's anger was too great now for him to give up.

Once more the lights in the Street of the Potters went out, and he settled down in silent solitude. After a long while—he had no idea of the time—he stood up and tried to walk a little, to get rid of the unpleasant tingling in his legs from sitting in one position. He turned into the first street on the right and, after twenty yards or so, into a narrow alley between two irregular rows of houses. As he walked, leaning on his staff, he saw a figure coming toward him from the Street of the Potters. In the light of the full moon—for him, dim—he made out a head of hair as fair as John's.

The man went quickly to a low door and gave three sharp raps, then a fourth, harder. A signal? Realizing that there might be another entrance to John's house from here, Lazarus hurried forward. As he did so, the man put his hand to his belt, as if to draw a knife.

"No!" cried Lazarus, who could not see the other's face in the dark. "I'm looking for a man named John. Are you he?"

At that moment, a bolt was drawn, the door opened, and a large man with a goatee appeared on the threshold. By the faint light from within, Lazarus recognized the first man, the person he had waited for three nights to see.

"What are you doing here?" Peter asked Lazarus in a low voice, as if afraid of being overheard.

"It is John I want to speak to, not you," said Lazarus.

"Leave us alone. You have no business here, and we have more important things to do than bother with you. Go away!"

"He's right," said John. "This is no place for you."

"I *must* speak to you," insisted Lazarus. "I've been looking for you for weeks, months. I've been all over the country, searching. Now that I've found you, I'm not going!"

"You heard what I said!" growled the big man. "We don't want you!"

Lazarus turned to John, but he lowered his eyes.

"Have you forgotten how you and the Galilean stayed in my house in Bethany?" he cried, reaching for the young man's arm. "Have you forgotten that I took you in when the people in Jerusalem wanted to kill you? I hid you for part of the night. I didn't hesitate, even though you were strangers. I did it because I thought it was my duty, just as I've always tried to help people in need. Have you forgotten that night? It's my turn to ask for help. You can't send me away."

"He's been here, knocking at the door, before you came— yesterday and the day before that," rumbled Peter. "Trying to worm his way in. Don't listen to him! They still haven't released Hosiah; how do you know this isn't the one who betrayed him? . . . I told you, it's time we moved to another place. Why will you never listen?"

"But he's right," said John softly. "I am in his debt."

"For goodness' sake take no notice of him! You know he's not one of us."

"Yes, I know," answered the young man.

"Who told you we were here?" cried the big man, grabbing Lazarus by the top of his tunic.

"Leave him alone," said John. "He may not actually have followed Jesus, but he did help us a long time ago, when some of the people we now accept were trembling with fear and nowhere to be found."

"I may not have followed Jesus," Lazarus said quickly, "but I was there on Golgotha! I stayed by the cross till the end, I saw him die. Which of you can say as much? None of you! I was the only one there! Where were you, his friends? I looked for you, to help him. What could I do alone? I looked for you, but you were hiding, hiding safely behind closed doors."

The big man released him, then after a pause said, "He's lying. He wasn't on Golgotha."

"Come with me," said John. "I hadn't intended to visit you for a long while yet, but never mind. Come with me, since that's what you want."

"You're crazy!" muttered the big man, his eyes flashing with anger. "I don't know why I let you do it. We'll all end up on the cross one day because of you."

"If we do, you know very well it won't be because of me," said John, showing Lazarus in.

In a low room lighted by two oil lamps, about a dozen men were sitting in a circle on the floor. They all looked up, and some of them seemed to recognize Lazarus, who wondered why they were hiding here. John led him to a smaller room, where, Lazarus noticed, the only window had been walled up.

The young man shut the door behind him. "Sit down," he said, indicating an old wooden bench between two mats that served as beds.

"Peter's afraid, but you can't blame him," he went on, putting down the canvas bag he had been carrying. "We're all afraid. Hosiah, one of our people, was arrested last week. Had I been here the last few days, I'd have opened the door to you."

"Where were you?" Lazarus asked.

"On the banks of the Jordan, looking for people who knew John the Baptist. I'm trying to write the story of Jesus. I'm looking for witnesses. Matthew the tax collector is doing the same."

"Why?"

"What Jesus said and did must be preserved. It should not disappear when we die. Look—I've already written all that!" He pointed to two rolls of papyrus lying on a table by a clay ink pot and a reed pen. "The people you saw in the other room make four or five copies of what I write, as I go along, and others will make more copies of the whole book when it's completed. That way, nothing will be lost or forgotten. . . . I'll soon reach your part of the story."

"Do you really think that ought to be included?" asked Lazarus.

"Of course. Your resurrection is the most wonderful of all the miracles. Everyone must know about it."

Lazarus nodded slowly. "I suppose it might seem wonderful," he said quietly, "to anyone who never met me."

135

As if he had not heard what Lazarus said, John lighted another lamp, placed it in a niche in the wall, and took from his bag a piece of rough parchment covered with writing, which he placed beside the rolls of papyrus.

"This is what I brought back from my journey," he said. "I found more than ten people in Enon and Salim who were willing to talk about John the Baptist. None of us was there when he baptized Jesus in the Jordan. The account I write tomorrow will probably go in the first chapter of the book. I often have to jump around like that, because every day I learn something new. That's why my progress is so slow.

"The people who have met Jesus are afraid to speak. They'll start by lying, saying they know nothing. Then, gradually, they let something out, mention a thing he did that surprised them, or a thing he said that they didn't understand but nevertheless remembered. If I'm very patient, I can nearly always get them to tell me what they know, and that's essential, because, although I was often with him, I realize there is much I still need to learn. Other people's impressions of him, the way they interpret what he said and did—all that is of value."

He brought a stool over and sat down facing Lazarus. "Actually," he said, smiling, "they want to talk. A few drive me away, and I've even been beaten, but mostly I get the feeling that it makes them happy to talk about him."

"Even here in Jerusalem?" asked Lazarus.

"It's different in Jerusalem. Here, everyone suspects everyone else. I have to hide and be careful. I never go out except at night and I speak only to people I know."

Lazarus had been observing him closely, and it seemed to

him that John looked older than when he and the Galilean had spent that night in Bethany. He was still thin, but his brow was furrowed now, and a beard had started to cover his cheeks and chin. His features had hardened, and his voice was no longer that of a boy. The one remaining sign of youth was the gentle expression in his eyes, which made him look naïve and vulnerable.

"Do you always write the truth?" asked Lazarus.

"What would be the point of lying?"

There was a pause.

"Will you say, for example, that none of your people were there on Golgotha?"

John shrugged and, after a moment, said yes, there was no reason why he should conceal it.

"And will you say that *I* was there?"

"Yes. Probably . . . certainly."

Lazarus, not convinced, shook his head. "I'd like to read your story when it's finished," he said.

Just then he was distracted by a babble of voices in the next room. He thought Peter and the rest must be praying together, as in the Temple. To whom were they praying, God or that Jesus of theirs? Lazarus listened, but could not make out the phrase they seemed to be repeating two or three times, like the verses of the Shema.

"Where is the Galilean?" he finally asked.

"Gone."

"Where?"

"Where neither you nor I can join him."

"That's what I thought you'd say," Lazarus sighed. "I'm not surprised. It's difficult for me to walk, yet I went all the way to Galilee to find him. Naturally, I didn't find him! Why? Because he never rose from the dead. You stole his body from the tomb three days after he died."

"If that's what you came here to tell me, you'd better go!" said John sternly. "You sound exactly like the people who want to silence and destroy us. Peter was right: this is no place for you!"

"But you always speak in riddles, all of you! Even with him, I couldn't understand half he said. What is this place where no one else can go? Tell me what you mean! I saw the stone that was rolled away from the empty tomb. Stop using words that make no sense! If you and the others didn't take his body and hide it to make people think he'd come back to life, tell me plainly where he is now."

"You don't believe in him despite what he did for you! If you did, I'd only have to say yes, he is risen from the dead, and you'd know it was the truth. . . . All the others in this house tonight believe in him, although he did not bring them back from the Great Sleep as he did you.

"They're waiting for me, and I will waste no more time on you. It's a pity you can't help us. I had hoped you could—that's why I let you in. But, unfortunately, though you know his power better than any of us, you don't believe, and accuse us of being liars and thieves."

"But look what he did with that power!" cried Lazarus. "Look at me! Can't you see my face, my body? Can't you smell the stench that comes from me? . . . Do you realize that because of him I can't eat, sleep or work anymore? I just wander, a beggar, a vagrant—I who used to work at the most honorable of trades. Because of him I can't make love anymore, and had to leave my wife, whom I once desired greatly.

Instead of faith, courage, love, and generosity, he's left me with despair, idleness, and hatred in my heart. You know him—tell me why he did this to me!"

John was silent. He looked at Lazarus now the way everyone else did.

"Do you realize that this is how I'll be forever and ever? That I'll never die, that the nightmare will never end? . . . You're writing his story—will you dare write that he reduced me to *this* forever?"

"What do you want of me?" asked John. "Do you think I have the power to change what he has done?"

"No. I just want to know why he did it. I didn't ask him for anything. I didn't ask him to bring me back to life. And *this* isn't life. Death is a thousand times better than this. Death is nothing, I'm not afraid of death. If only I knew how to get back to it!"

The oil lamp in the niche shed a yellow light on the young man's forehead and cheek. It seemed to Lazarus that John was regarding him exactly the way the Galilean's mother had. They were all alike; there was no point in trying.

"Don't worry. I'm going," Lazarus said. "You don't care what becomes of me. You're as incapable of helping me as the rest."

"As I said before," answered John, "I have neither the power nor the will to undo what he has done."

"I know," said Lazarus. "That's not what I am asking! . . . But why won't you explain? What are you trying to hide? Who else but you can explain it to me? If there's some reason why it should have happened to me, tell me, and I promise I'll go away."

They looked at each other. John was the first to lower his eyes.

"He did it so that you might bear witness," he said softly.

"Bear witness to what?"

"That you might bear witness forever that he truly is the son of God."

"I don't understand," said Lazarus.

"Anyone who sees you as you are now is bound to believe in him. They can see you exactly as you were when he snatched you from the tomb five days after you died. They can see the unmistakable marks of death on your face and body, can smell the odor of death on you, and must believe, because what they see is beyond question. Had he brought you back as you were before, the same as the rest of us, with your strong shoulders, your former health and energy, no one who saw you would believe that you had risen from the grave. As you are, they are forced to believe that you have returned from the realm of the dead, and that only the son of God could have brought you back."

"Do you realize what you are saying?"

"Yes. Simply that you are proof, Lazarus—tangible, indestructible proof. I knew it the moment I touched you in Bethany on the day of your resurrection, when I helped support you as you tottered at the entrance to the tomb, your limbs still wrapped, your head still covered. I felt your icy body, smelled the damp smell of corruption despite the fragrant oils and aloes, and I understood."

"But if he really was the son of God, why did he need such proof?" asked Lazarus, appalled, incredulous.

"He must have decided that an indisputable sign, different from all his other miracles, was necessary."

"You mean to tell me," murmured Lazarus, "that he did it to prove his own power, so that people would believe in him and worship him?"

"No, not that! I, too, sometimes thought that he sought glory for himself. But I'm certain now that that's not true."

"But why me? I who helped him?" whispered Lazarus. "And what sort of *God* is it who, in order to be recognized, is willing to destroy forever someone who never did any harm?"

He paused, staring into space. An icy chill enveloped him.

"It hasn't worked, anyway," he said faintly. "People fear me. They make fun of me, they run away from me. I'm an invalid, a freak. No one really believes that Jesus brought me out of the Great Sleep, no one—not even Jair, the blind man from the Pool of Siloam. It's all been for nothing. He's plunged me into this horror for nothing."

"You're wrong. There are many who, because of you, are beginning to think."

Lazarus shook his head, eyes fixed on a distance beyond the fair face and the gray wall in front of him. "So there's no way out," he whispered.

"Yes," answered John, "there is one. But no one can help you find it. You'll discover it for yourself when you come to believe in him. And when that happens, you'll rejoice that he chose you to play such a wonderful part."

THREE

Jair did not leave Jacob's place until the merchants had shut up their shops and the sky over Jerusalem had started to grow dark. Then he slipped out into the empty street. He could feel the first coolness falling over the city. Night came quickly now; summer was nearly over.

Looking up, he saw the torches of the Roman soldiers, who were taking up their positions on carefully chosen rooftops throughout the city. Ever since two more of their number had been stabbed near the Temple during Pentecost, they had been keeping armed watch over the streets in groups of four or five. But far from calming things down, this, like their guard over the Temple, only provoked further incidents, and crosses were more and more frequently raised on Golgotha.

Jair quickened his pace. Instead of taking the lane that

went along the Tyropoeon valley, which was always full of soldiers, he made for the Pool of Siloam by way of darker, yet less dangerous, side streets. Hugging the walls, he went through tortuous alleys, which the Romans still avoided.

The main thing was to keep clear of patrols. After nightfall, soldiers stopped all Jews and searched them for arms. What would they do if they found what he was hiding under his cloak? The Romans, alarmed by the consequences of having crucified an alleged messiah, would be suspicious of anything remotely concerning the words or deeds of Jesus. People said that the procurator himself, following the lead of the Sanhedrin, had recently ordered the arrest of anyone found speaking of the Galilean, repeating his words, or telling of his miracles. Jair no longer dared say aloud the prayer the Galilean had taught on Mount Scopus.

As the sky above filled with stars, Jair wondered what Lazarus would do when he told him his news. Would he turn away in silence? Would he lose his temper again? The more he thought about it, the more Jair felt that what he was proposing to do was pointless. For eight weeks since he had met John, Lazarus had been dejected, sullen, and refused to talk about the Galilean. What was the use of persisting? The last time Jair had tried to talk to him, he had succeeded only in infuriating him. "I'm tired of your kindness, your generosity!" Lazarus had shouted.

Then Lazarus went away, leaving Jair alone by the Pool of Siloam. When he did not return after a few days, Jair was worried, and, though he did not consider himself particularly attached to Lazarus, found himself setting off through the streets of Jerusalem to look for him.

For some unknown reason, he could not do without him

now, despite Lazarus's endless silences and his own occasional doubts about the Bethany resurrection. And yet he isn't any use to me, Jair had thought as he went in search of him—on the steps, near Herod's Palace, and on the Hill of Evil Counsel. On the contrary, he makes my blood run cold.

Perhaps it was because Lazarus, too, had been the subject of a miracle, and thus was one of those in whom Jesus had taken a personal interest. But that explanation did not satisfy Jair.

After four days, convinced that his search was senseless, Jair had gone again to Keturah's and spent the night stretched out on her massive body, clasped in her clammy arms.

The next morning, inexplicably, there was Lazarus, sitting in his shady corner at the bottom of the steps leading down to the Pool of Siloam.

Jair had asked no questions. Carefully concealing his delight, he merely shared his bread with him at midday, as before.

Since then, he had not mentioned the Galilean in Lazarus's presence.

As he went down the steps, it occurred to him that what he really wanted was to provoke Lazarus. The man's silence exasperated him. I don't care if I do make him angry, he thought. Let him insult me. That would be better than nothing.

It was dark by the time he reached the pool, and he had to pick his way between the shapes huddled on the ground under the colonnades. Many of the men were snoring. A woman groaned in her sleep. Jair accidentally stepped on something soft, and there was a volley of angry curses. At the bottom he nearly tripped over a shapeless heap of rags. Carefully, he made his way to the wall on the far side of the

147

pool, where he found Lazarus, as usual, sitting huddled in a small recess. Making sure not to damage his roll of parchment, Jair wrapped himself in his cloak and lay down beside him.

"It's starting to get cold at night now," he said.

"Yes," Lazarus replied.

Next morning, Lazarus watched as Jair woke with the first rays of the sun. Many of the sick were already up, bathing their sores and diseased limbs in the muddy water. Some shouted, quarreled; a blind man who did not get out of the way got his head split open with a stick.

The first thing Jair did was check that the precious scroll was still safe under his cloak. Then, as was his custom on waking, he looked up to where a few lavender streaks were still visible against the pale-blue sky and silently repeated the prayer from Mount Scopus.

"We'll have good weather," he said when he was finished. "It won't rain this year on the Feast of Tabernacles, in two days."

Lazarus remembered that it had poured torrents in Bethany on the twenty-fifth day of Tishri almost a year ago, when they were harvesting the grapes and the olives. He had a fleeting vision of Susannah, drenched, in her embroidered red gown. She was gathering olives in a big basket at the foot of the hill behind the house. Her hair and its braided ribbons were soaked, and the *sikra* with which she had reddened her lips and cheeks ran down her face in streams. However hard he struggled against her image, it kept returning to him with cruel clarity. The slightest thing was enough to bring it back, at any moment, day or night. . . .

"Will you do me a favor?" asked Jair, interrupting these painful thoughts. "You can read. Will you read something for me?"

As soon as he saw the roll of parchment, Lazarus knew what it was. His first impulse was to refuse. He had made it clear that he did not want to hear anything more about the Galilean. But his curiosity to know whether John had told the truth, as he had promised eight weeks ago, was too strong. Jair explained, cautiously, that he had been given the writings by his new friend, Jacob, and that they contained the story of Jesus.

"I know," said Lazarus. "John told me when I met him at his house."

And to Jair's amazement, he began, without protest or complaint, to undo the long scroll, which was made of papyrus leaves sewn together. The writing was poor and irregular; it looked as if the copyist had done these chapters in a hurry, perhaps afraid of being discovered. Lazarus looked first for the account of his own resurrection, but parts of the text were obviously missing, and he could not find it. In passing, he noticed a number of words he did not understand and thought: John is not clear and straightforward even when he writes. He skimmed a series of short chapters, some of them broken off in mid-sentence. Finally he came to Jesus' arrest and his appearance before Annas and Caiaphas.

Then he reached the crucifixion.

The letters blurred and the lines kept shaking before his eyes, but Lazarus read eagerly, in a low voice, for himself.

Several details were correct: the words written on the cross over Jesus' head, the soldiers drawing lots for his tunic, the

149

sword thrust in his side. . . . So John had found someone to tell him about the Galilean's death. Who? Mary, the mother, or the other woman in black?

Lazarus read on, and soon it was all too clear. Not only had John failed to mention that he, Lazarus, was there that day on the Hill of the Skull, but, worse, he had had the audacity to write that the Galilean, just before he died, seeing his mother standing by with the disciple "whom he loved," had said to her, "Woman, behold thy son!"

And who was this virtuous disciple who, to complete the lie, was afterward supposed to have taken Mary "unto his own home," as a son might take his mother? Everyone who knew the Galilean knew that of all the band of beggars who followed him around, and whom he often seemed to despise, the only one he felt good will or even friendship toward was John, the youngest. John, the most attentive.

Lazarus rested the scroll on his lap. Such shameless falsehood, though shocking, was also a source of satisfaction to him: it proved that these messiah worshipers were liars and probably thieves.

"I'm sorry to have to tell you that this is full of lies," he said, handing the scroll back to Jair. "I know, because I was at Golgotha myself when the Galilean was crucified. I saw what really happened."

When Haggai woke on the first day of the Feast of Tabernacles, he could see from the position of the sun in the sky that it was already near the third hour.

He could not understand why he, once in the habit of rising before dawn, lately had been finding it so hard to get out of bed. This morning again he felt weak, feverish, heavy-limbed. He went and looked out the window. Mount Gareb, facing his house, was covered with tents and booths, just as it had been during Passover. Pilgrims had arrived during the night, enough to fill the courts of the Temple and the streets of Jerusalem. Fortunately, no one would reproach him for his absence from the opening ceremonies.

He blamed himself, though, for missing the morning procession. Only last year, despite the pouring rain that had flooded some of the lower parts of the city and soaked his own vestments through and through, he had officiated at the high altar, facing the open Nicador Gate; he had slit the throats of three lambs with his own hand. But since the beginning of his illness, a week ago, these surges of heat had numbed his limbs and brain, made him alternately shiver and sweat, and he had been good for nothing.

Today, more than ever, his helplessness distressed him. The Feast of Tabernacles, commemorating the days when the Jews were "mere wanderers on the face of the earth," was especially important to him.

He walked heavily to the pitcher on the other side of the room, poured water over his naked body, and slowly rubbed himself from head to foot with marjoram. Then he sat in front of the polished-metal mirror belonging to his wife Elizabeth, put a few drops of fragrant oil on his head, and combed his hair and beard with a golden comb. Before he dressed, he gazed at his reflection. Since the beginning of summer his face had changed. It had become mournful; his nose had grown longer and more prominent, his cheeks more sunken, the furrows on his brow deeper.

His doctors had tried various remedies to cure this lethargy that immobilized his body and mind and made it impossible for him to perform his normal duties as a priest and leading member of the Sanhedrin. All their attempts were useless. He ate whole pots of honey every day; he let himself be bled; fig plasters were applied to his chest; he swallowed countless potions—all in vain. His strange malady persisted. No matter how much incense he burned or how many costly sacrifices he offered up every evening in the Temple, nothing changed. There was no pain, except for an occasional headache. Only the overwhelming heat and the fatigue.

Bringing the mirror close, he could see the new white in his hair, especially at the temples, and in his thick beard. "I'm getting old," he said aloud. "That's why I'm ill. I don't have the resistance I used to have."

He went over to the cup that stood by the pitcher of water and rinsed his mouth. He would soon be thirty-five; his father was dead before that, he thought.

Slowly he put on his white linen tunic, his embroidered belt, and his priestly conical headdress. Still feeling ill, he went out to the balcony and descended the outside staircase to the courtyard. He hated thinking about getting old, about dying. The thought that someday he would no longer exist sent a chill down his spine.

He found his daughter Yona embroidering the hem of a gown and bent to kiss her. When his lips touched her brow, she did not respond: she was still cross from the quarrel they had had the evening before over Joktan, a mere Sanhedrin scribe whom she had gone to meet secretly on the Mount of Olives two days ago. Haggai pretended not to notice her coldness and moved away without comment. He would keep her under lock and key until she forgot that insignificant young puppy. Her girlish anger would fade in the end. The wisest course, for the present at least, was not to upset her further, even over something as important as the respect a daughter owed her father.

When Haggai reached the Tyropoeon valley, he found himself in the midst of a crowd of pilgrims chanting Psalm 118: "The stone which the builders refused is become the head stone of the corner . . ." Luckily, they made way for him when they saw his white tunic and priestly vestments. As he went down toward the Pool of Siloam, he noticed with relief that the Romans, probably afraid of being overwhelmed, as they had been during Passover, when two of them were killed, had assembled on the rooftops instead, to oversee the procession from a safe distance.

He was glad, too, not to meet a single legionary on duty in the streets. The procurator must have realized how dangerous it was for his men to expose themselves to the crowds on holy days. With luck, this week's ceremonies, like those of Yom Kippur a fortnight ago, would take place without incident, despite the three armed centuries deployed along the porticoes around the Temple esplanade. Was the time approaching when Roman and Jew, weary of crucifixions and massacres, would be content to observe one another from a distance?

Haggai hoped that reason would prevail at last, despite Rabbi Shammai and the doctors of the Law, the rash scribes and Pharisees, whose crude pronouncements only served to inflame people against the foreign invader.

The nearer he came to the tower of Siloam, the hotter his head was, the dizzier he felt. Now he could hear the lutes and cymbals of the Levite musicians, and, about a hundred yards ahead, at the foot of the steps, he saw the diadem of the high priest. Caiaphas, bearing the golden pitcher before him, was at the head of a procession that included every member of the Sanhedrin.

Haggai joined Elihu, Samuel, and Zerah, his friends on the Council. They greeted him respectfully, showing they understood why he had not been present at the morning prayers and sacrifices. No one seemed inclined to blame him for being late. Only Bartholomew, walking in front of him, saw fit to turn around and say, maliciously, that the Sanhedrin was grateful Father Haggai had decided to join them.

Haggai made no reply. One day, probably too late, Bartholomew and the Pharisees would bitterly regret their words, their behavior.

When the procession reached the pool, Caiaphas descended the nine steps to the water. The seventy members of the Sanhedrin and the priests, scribes, and doctors of the Law ranged themselves beneath the colonnades above the stairs. People crowded the surrounding roofs and the ramparts of the ancient city of David to watch the ceremony.

Caiaphas, attended by a Levite, knelt to fill the golden pitcher with holy water. Choir and musicians fell silent as the old man recited Psalm 118 in his quavering voice. The Temple servants had, as usual, got rid of the cripples and beggars who lived around the pool. Haggai, standing at the top of the steps, wondered how so many sick people could cram themselves into so small a space. As his eyes wandered over the wall surrounding the pool below, he noticed a shadow stirring in a dark recess. It looked like a man reclining on one elbow. Why had the Temple servants left him there? This

154

evening he would make sure to tell Daniel, their chief, that they had done their work badly.

The man, probably a cripple, moved nearer the light, and, strangely, did not seem to care about being noticed. Then, in a slanting ray of sunlight, Haggai saw his face, and at the same time caught a familar whiff of corruption and rancid oil. He would have recognized that face anywhere: it was engraved in his mind until his dying day!

Perspiration streamed from him. It's the heat in my head giving me hallucinations, he thought, averting his eyes from the recess in the wall. I should not have come.

He looked at the high priest, silent now at the foot of the steps. Caiaphas, still supported by the Levite, leaned over the pool. Slowly the pitcher was lowered into the dirty water.

It's not possible, thought Haggai. Mattheos killed Lazarus months ago; he swore to me he stabbed him many times in the street in Bethany!

He had to look again, to reassure himself that it was his illness making him see things. But an irrational fear prevented him from turning his eyes toward the dark recess in the wall.

The onyx pieces on the shoulders of the high priest's tunic glittered in the sun, and Haggai's head began to spin. Zerah was standing beside him. To keep himself from falling, Haggai clutched his friend's arm.

"What's the matter?" Zerah asked.

"Nothing," said Haggai. "I just don't feel quite well yet."

He stood straight again and, as Caiaphas withdrew the full pitcher from the water, forced himself to look at the wall. This time, all he could see was a shadowy hollow that seemed empty.

155

But he could have sworn he saw Lazarus lying there! . . .

As Caiaphas, bearing the holy water, led the procession back to the Temple, Haggai even wondered if Lazarus, the being suspended between life and death, had ever existed outside his own troubled imagination.

Toward the eleventh hour, the sounds of the great feast reached Haggai as he reclined in his inner courtyard. His wife sat facing him, as did Yona, still sullen. Against his will, Haggai started thinking again about the vision of death at the Pool of Siloam. He could still smell the decay coming from Lazarus's gray skin. To divert himself, he decided to go out again, ignoring the fire in his head and the dizziness.

In addition to this strange anguish that gripped him, he also felt guilty for not attending the evening ceremonies.

Shivering, he put on his heavy winter cloak. As the servants shut the door behind him, he wondered whether he ought to go straight back to the Pool of Siloam and find out what really had been there. But no, the poor and the sick would be back in their usual places for the night, and he would not be able to see anything among all those bodies in the dark. This is absurd, he thought. Why do I attach so much importance to the vision of a fever?

He reached the Court of the Women just as the four great candelabra were being lighted on the steps leading to the high altar. There was such a crowd milling around under the watchful eyes of the Romans atop the colonnades that he gave up hope of joining Samuel and Zerah, who were probably by the entrance to the sanctuary, beyond the basin for ablutions. He regretted not being able to appear before his friends—

156

and before his opponents—in the Sanhedrin, to show them that despite his illness he had come to take part in the ceremony of the candles.

A dozen Temple servants on ladders were busy lighting the branches of the tall, solid-gold candelabra. Watching their clumsy efforts, Haggai wished he had complained to Daniel about the man they had failed to turn away from the Pool of Siloam before the arrival of the high priest. These incompetents needed to be taught a lesson.

But no—on reflection, it was better that he had done nothing; no one else seemed to have noticed Lazarus, and he probably had been mistaken. Besides, under the circumstances, it would be unwise for a man in his position to make accusations. . . .

When all seven branches of the four candelabra had been lighted, Haggai remembered how, the year before, Jesus of Nazareth had looked at the flames and told the listeners around him that he was "the light of the world." Haggai, standing on the steps only a few yards away, had heard every word: "He that follows me shall not walk in darkness, but shall have the light of life." The blasphemy had shown how great a danger this fanatic was to the Jewish people. And was Jesus not supposed to have said the same thing again a little while later, in Bethany, by Lazarus's tomb?

Haggai gazed at the spectacle as the musicians took their places on the stairs by the open Nicador Gate. Torches in the Court of the Women illuminated the bronze and marble columns; gold and silver glittered on the massive doors; the newly hewn stones of the walls were white as snow. Costly metal spikes, set thick on the roof of the sanctuary to keep the birds away, gleamed red and yellow, like a forest at sunset. In one of the smaller courtyards, pilgrims went up one by one to a few cured lepers, to touch or kiss limbs made whole by the grace of the Almighty.

The trumpets let out their long monotonous call, and cymbals, lutes, and tabors, placed along the fifteen steps, began to play. Then, in accordance with tradition, people began to dance and wave their arms among the flaming torches, casting a multitude of shadows on the white walls. The shadows swept over the pillars, too, mingling, writhing, and swelling, right to the top of the carved balustrades.

Haggai, despite his anguish and his fevered brow, felt better as he watched the people proclaiming their faith in this most magnificent of holy places. Yes, he thought, he would fight, as long as he lived, to protect the Temple.

Just before the end of the festivities, Haggai left. He walked home slowly, because his legs were stiff and painful. The joy he had experienced in the Court of the Women soon faded, to be replaced by the old dread. On the street leading to the forum and Herod's Palace, he wondered if he would die soon of this malady that increasingly left him feeble and dazed. His fear, his morbid visions, his constant desire to lie down— were these not signs heralding his end?

He slept badly that night, waking up repeatedly in a cold sweat. In intermittent dreams he saw himself as a child, going into his parents' bedroom to find his father naked, dead, and his mother weeping as she anointed the swollen corpse with aloes and myrrh. This image, surfacing from his memory, merged with the even more frightening image of Lazarus summoned from the darkness by a pale shaft of sunlight.

At dawn Haggai rose, certain that his dreams were connected with the vision at the Pool of Siloam. He recited the

Shema, praying to Yahweh to deliver him from his black thoughts. Then he consumed eight spoonfuls of honey and, resisting an urge to get back in bed, put on an old tunic and an ancient brown cloak. On his head he draped a large kaffiyeh, which came down to his shoulders, and fastened it with two headbands. Without his official garb, the priest would be anonymous, like any other Jew in Jerusalem for the Feast of Tabernacles.

He went down and found Mattheos in the servants' room. Without explanation, he told him to come with him at once. They crossed half the city, Haggai forcing himself to hurry despite the weakness in his legs. As they walked, he kept looking at his servant, bought twenty-three years ago in the market at Tyre by Haggai's father, on one of his journeys. Had loyal, trusted Mattheos lied to him, and if so, why? Haggai knew that the Nazarene's words and miracles still affected people, especially the very poor, but he refused to believe that they had penetrated into his own house and influenced an illiterate slave brought long ago, in chains, from a distant country. But if such was indeed the case, Haggai would know how to act with the proper severity.

As he had hoped, they reached the Pool of Siloam before it had been cleared for the arrival of the high priest on the second day of the feast. It was just after sunrise, and many of the usual inhabitants were still asleep, sprawled under the pillars of the portico, on the steps, and even around the pool. Haggai drew his kaffiyeh across his nose and mouth and told Mattheos to do the same. Stepping over the mounds of bodies, they skirted the rectangle of water and made for the wall on the far side.

Haggai stopped a few feet from the dark recess and saw

at once, beside another half-recumbent form, the blind man who had been cured at Siloam. He knew him well, having met and questioned him only a few days after the Nazarene restored his sight. The thought that he might be here to meet Lazarus made Haggai tremble.

The man sat by the low wall, apparently counting the handful of coins set out on the ground in front of him. It was definitely Jair. Haggai could remember their meeting quite clearly: the simple fellow, though somewhat frightened, could not refrain from telling the representative of the Sanhedrin that he believed Jesus of Nazareth was the Messiah. . . . It occurred to Haggai that, instead of being in such a hurry to silence Naham, the overtalkative cripple from Capernaum, Elihu and Zerah might have done better to turn their attention to Jair.

He went closer, to see the face of the man beside Jair with his back half-turned. He found himself hoping that it would not be Lazarus.

Jair looked up, then said something to his companion, who moved slightly—but enough for Haggai to identify the man beyond all possible doubt. No, he had not been dreaming before!

Haggai turned to Mattheos, who was gaping at Lazarus. "I swear I followed your instructions," the servant whispered. "I stabbed him three times. The blade went up to the hilt, in his neck, in his stomach, I swear it! I killed him! He cannot be alive!"

Haggai said nothing. He was assessing the gravity of what he saw: the obvious friendship of two men who had both been the subject of miracles, a friendship for all to see in the heart of Jerusalem—and for the greater glory of the Nazarene.

He sent Mattheos home to wait for him: they would have another talk about how Lazarus had been "killed" in the streets of Bethany. Then, after another glance at Jair and Lazarus sitting quietly side by side, he went to tell his friend Zerah of his discovery.

On the morning of the fourth day of the Feast of Tabernacles, at sunrise, when the Temple servants had not yet moved the people from the Pool of Siloam, four armed guards came for Lazarus and Jair.

They seized them, bound them, and led them away through the streets of the lower city.

No matter how earnestly Jair protested that he and Lazarus had done nothing wrong, he received no answer. He remembered how Peter's friend Hosiah had been missing since early summer, and thought uneasily that perhaps he himself was being arrested—to be made to confess how and where he met with Jacob, Stephen, and the rest, the ever-increasing numbers who assembled to talk about Jesus, to remember him, and to read the writings of Matthew and John.

He noticed that Lazarus seemed indifferent to what was happening. Lazarus had let himself be dragged away without a word or the slightest show of resistance. It's good he knows nothing about where I go when I leave him each evening, Jair thought. He'd be sure to give it away.

Their captors took them down the sloping streets of the lower city to the other side of the Tyropoeon valley, through the dyers' quarter, and on to the high priest's house, which was by the ramparts close to Herod's Palace and served as a prison for people waiting to appear before the Sanhedrin. After crossing a large paved courtyard full of trees and exotic plants, Jair and Lazarus, escorted by five armed men on duty as Caiaphas's bodyguards, were taken down a dark stairway that led deep underground, and along a passageway lighted every twenty yards by torches set in iron rings. The walls oozed from the dampness.

Their guards stopped, and Jair could hear moans coming from up ahead. As his eyes grew accustomed to the fitful torchlight, he made out, through an open door, a post with ropes attached to it, and a cavity in the wall, for the salt and vinegar used to stanch wounds after a flogging.

He wondered if he would have the courage to remain silent under the whip.

They were pushed on again, past an old cistern. Jair, who had learned to interpret sounds when he was blind, knew that that was where the groans were coming from. At the bottom of a well shaft, a condemned man was probably awaiting his final punishment.

He had no time to reflect on this, because almost at once he and Lazarus were thrust into separate dungeons, and the doors, of solid wood and iron, were bolted shut behind them.

Jair found himself in total darkness once more. As if he were blind again. He screamed. He must be set free! He must have light again!

There was no answer. He was alone with his fear.

For a long time he stood motionless. Then he took a few steps forward, his arms outstretched to avoid obstacles, just as he used to do before the miracle. His cell was small, and his fingers soon came to the corner formed by two cold, damp walls. He slumped down and sat cross-legged on the floor.

What had he done wrong, what mistake had he made, to be imprisoned like this? He had taken the strictest precautions when he went to see his new friends. He had stopped saying the Mount Scopus prayer aloud and never mentioned Jesus anywhere but in Jacob's house. . . .

Cold, he hunched his knees up to his chest for warmth. He thought of Lazarus's indifference when the guards seized them. Was it all the same to Lazarus—imprisonment, suffering, perhaps death? Lazarus certainly would not hesitate to say what he thought about Jesus. Jair hoped he would at least keep quiet about John's writings.

Drops of water dripped on the ground nearby. The sound soon became unbearable. Jair realized, with horror, that it would keep him awake: he would lie sleepless in the dark, until he went mad.

He shut his eyes to avoid seeing the darkness.

To give himself courage, he thought about Jesus. In particular, about his death, which Lazarus, after reading John's account, had finally described to him. There was no comparison between the sufferings on the cross, Jair told himself, and his own mere loss of liberty and light. Why could he not be like Jesus? . . .

He must be out of his mind, to ask such a question! Was not Jesus the Messiah? Jair, an ordinary man, poor, frightened, and not so long ago blind, could not compare himself with the Messiah.

Endless hours went by. Finally he managed to forget the sound of the water and sink into a kind of half-sleep.

The sudden noise of an iron grill being opened somewhere in the corridor roused him from his torpor. He heard footsteps on the damp floor. He opened his eyes, sat up. The ruddy light of a torch, approaching, showed beneath his door, revealed the earthen floor, his feet, his legs, his tunic, his arms.

Then the clinking of keys faded in the distance, and the light disappeared.

Jair lost all sense of time, and when his door opened at last, he felt as if he had spent an entire week shut up in the dark. He did not know that the Feast of Tabernacles was still going on in the streets of Jerusalem and the courtyard of the Temple, and that only a day and a half had passed since his arrest.

He opened his eyes. In the uncertain light of a torch, he could see the outline of a man sitting on a stool facing him. The visitor slowly became clearer to him. Under a large black cloak, which he had thrown back, the man wore the white tunic of a priest. Around his neck and hanging on his chest was the scarf worn by members of the Sanhedrin, and on his head were the turban and kaffiyeh that dignitaries of the Council used on nonceremonial occasions.

"Have you come to set me free?" asked Jair, recognizing

his visitor. "There was no need to have me arrested just to ask me more questions." He tried not to sound belligerent.

The priest regarded him with a grim, piercing gaze that boded no good.

"I told you everything I knew when you came to Siloam to see me, soon after the miracle," Jair went on, almost whining.

Haggai said that he had other questions to ask, different questions, infinitely more important than the ones asked before.

Disappointed by Jair's answers, Haggai sat on a stone bench in Caiaphas's garden and pondered how best to conduct the impending interrogation of Lazarus.

How could Lazarus be made to confess that he and his friend had joined forces to make the people of Jerusalem believe that the Nazarene was the true Messiah?

Haggai looked at the door of the audience chamber to which he had had Lazarus taken. He did not like the idea of this encounter; the prospect of confronting that living corpse again revived the thoughts of mortality that had been haunting him for days. And why had he been unable to get more out of Jair? What had made the wretch suddenly so cautious? It was a mistake to have let him sit for so long, he thought. I should have questioned him as soon as he was arrested. He's too frightened now to tell the truth. . . .

He tried to imagine Lazarus waiting for him, in chains. He pictured the withered, stony face, and again smelled the odor of decay. It seemed to cling to Haggai, from the moment the ray of light had shown that sinister countenance in the gloom at Siloam.

166

If only Jair had admitted the truth, instead of swearing that he and Lazarus never spoke of the Nazarene, either among themselves or to third parties. Then Haggai could have avoided this interview. Of course, he would have Jair flogged. But how seriously would his enemies in the Sanhedrin take a confession obtained by torture?

Haggai looked at the great tubs overflowing with greenery and faded flowers. He shivered. His illness was not over. He should have followed the advice of his doctors and stayed in bed. If he kept on like this, he would never get better.

He turned again toward the open door. This meeting was, after all, only the logical consequence of the arrests he had ordered. Unpleasant as it might be, he must face it. He rose, mustered his courage, and entered the audience chamber.

The first thing he heard in that hall, with its painted walls and fluted pillars, was the rasping breath that had stuck in his memory ever since his visit to Bethany. Lazarus, ankles chained, stood on the other side of the room, by the empty seat of the high priest. His head was bowed. Haggai noticed that his tunic was coming apart at the seams, revealing a hollow, wrinkled chest. His hair and beard were dull as ashes; his shoulders, arms, and ankles looked as brittle as dry tinder.

Haggai, to show he was not afraid, sat down on a stool not far from him.

Then Lazarus looked up, and Haggai saw again the gaunt head, the furrowed brow, the look of suffering and dismay that had impressed him so strongly in Bethany.

Haggai asked if Lazarus remembered him.

After a pause Lazarus said, in a voice that seemed to come from the depths of his chest, that he remembered him very well.

Haggai hesitated, not knowing how to begin. Then he decided to go straight to the point. "How did you come to know Jair?" he asked.

"I was looking for another person who had been the subject of a miracle," Lazarus slowly replied. "So I went to Siloam to see him."

"For what purpose?"

"I hoped that he would know where the Galilean was hiding, since the Galilean was supposed to have risen from the dead."

"And did Jair tell you?"

"No. He didn't know."

Haggai was relieved to find that Lazarus could speak more easily now than when they first met in Bethany. He no longer separated his words into syllables, and, though he still talked slowly, his mouth did not seem so stiff. At least Haggai would be able to understand what he said.

"Why did you want to see the Galilean again?" he asked.

There was a long pause as Lazarus's eyes wandered vacantly over the wall behind Haggai. "I wanted him to explain," he said, almost in a whisper.

"Explain what?"

"Why he brought me back from the grave, when death was a thousand times better than this half-life."

The priest drew back, to avoid the icy breath he felt each time Lazarus spoke.

"You mean you would prefer death to . . . *this*?" he asked.

"Yes," said Lazarus simply.

It was Haggai's turn now to be silent. He was disconcerted by what Lazarus had said. How could anyone long for the grave, for the cold and darkness of death?

"Do you reproach the Nazarene for bringing you back from the Great Sleep?" he asked.

"I didn't ask him for anything. He brought me out of the darkness only in order to make people believe in him, worship him."

"But you yourself do not believe in him?"

"He was a liar, interested only in his fame," Lazarus answered mildly. "And all his friends were liars, too, and thieves."

"He brought you back to life and yet you do not believe in him!"

Lazarus slowly shook his head and turned away, as if he did not want to say more.

Haggai had been wrong to think that this miserable wretch would speak the truth. "You're like the rest of them," he shouted. "You believe he was the Messiah, and say so to everyone you meet!"

Lazarus said nothing.

"Do you realize I can have you flogged to get the truth out of you?" Haggai was infuriated by the man's indifference. "Do you realize I can have you put to death tomorrow, if I choose?"

No, it was a mistake for him to lose his temper. He stood up and walked back and forth for a while to calm himself. At the open door he looked out at the fountain in the middle of Caiaphas's garden. The ground swayed beneath his feet and a wave of heat flooded his forehead. He would get nowhere if he lost control of himself. These interrogations were not going well.

Haggai steadied himself and took a deep breath. What would I look like, he thought, bringing these two before the Sanhedrin to say what they are saying now?

He waited for his dizziness to pass. Then, disregarding the smell, which seemed to work its way into his own body, he approached Lazarus. "Is it because you suffer so much physically that you deny he was the Messiah?" he asked.

"He was not the Messiah," said Lazarus with a sigh.

"Does your friend Jair think he was?"

"We never discuss it."

"What do you discuss, then? What do you do, at Siloam?"

Lazarus raised his head and looked around vaguely, as if bored. Haggai controlled his anger. "I want you to tell me what you do together," he said sharply. "I know you are together all the time."

"We do nothing," said Lazarus. "What do you think we do? . . . I don't speak. I sit in a recess in the wall, day and night. . . . Most of the time, he sits there with me."

Haggai felt again that the man was not lying. What he said confirmed what Jair had said.

"No one ever comes and asks to hear your story?"

"Few in Jerusalem know who we are. Few remember the Galilean and his miracles. What he did for me was useless. And those who remember Lazarus the son of Chaim, risen from the grave, are too afraid to approach us at the Pool of Siloam, in public, where everyone can see them."

Haggai sat on the stool again, his chest burning, his back cold as ice. "Aren't you afraid I might keep you in prison for years?" he asked tonelessly.

"Do as you like," said Lazarus. "It makes no difference where I stay."

The priest shook his head. "I was wrong to think that there was any point in seeing you again." But, not wanting to end the interview thus, he got up and approached Lazarus again.

Studying him from head to foot, taking in the ravaged face and feeble, malodorous body, he almost understood, for a moment, why Lazarus would not believe the Nazarene was the Messiah.

Noticing the dirty rag around the prisoner's neck, Haggai recalled that Mattheos was supposed to have stabbed the man in the throat. If his servant had obeyed orders, as he claimed, there had to be some mark.

"Remove that bandage!" Haggai ordered.

When Lazarus obeyed, the priest saw a deep, dry, open wound, its pallid edges gaping like a pair of lips.

"What is that?" he cried with a grimace of disgust.

"A thief attacked me one morning in the street, in Bethany. He cut my throat."

Mattheos had not been lying!

"How is it you did not die of such a wound?"

Lazarus bowed his head and left the question unanswered.

It's impossible, thought Haggai, moving away. He couldn't still be alive. . . .

"Take off your tunic," he commanded.

Lazarus obeyed, revealing two more gashes, one between his ribs and the other in his stomach. The wound in the chest showed layers of colorless tissue. . . .

Now something frightened the priest even more than the thought of death.

Lazarus left his dungeon that evening.

He had been lying on the floor, floating in his pseudo slumber, when a guard came and told him to take his things and go.

Lazarus picked up his cloak and went out without asking for any explanation. Again he passed the well. This time no groans rose from it. He went through the dim, torch-lit passages and climbed—almost reluctantly—up the steps into the fading light of an autumn evening. Looking for his friend, he scanned the high priest's garden, which was filled with a profusion of foliage and flowers. Jair was not there.

Perhaps Jair, carried away by his fervor, had said that he believed the Galilean was the Messiah. That would mean they would keep him in prison a long time. Lazarus refused to think of a worse possibility. It was not likely that the authorities would start killing every idiot who took a dead magician for a deity. . . . But why should a member of the Sanhedrin have bothered to imprison them both? Unless crucifying the Galilean had not been enough. Unless they had to persecute everyone whose life he had touched.

The Feast of Tabernacles was drawing to a close, and the streets of Jerusalem were still full of people. Lazarus had difficulty making his way through the crowds of pilgrims and peddlers to the Pool of Siloam, though it was not far. When he reached the top of the steps leading down to the water, he found himself hoping that Jair would be waiting for him in the usual place, leaning against the wall by the recess. . . .

Jair was not.

Lazarus picked his way over the bodies of beggars and cripples huddled together and half asleep. He went back to his recess in the wall beyond the pool and curled up there, alone.

He could not see how such destitute men as Jair and himself could be regarded by anyone as a threat. The Galilean's enemies were, in fact, doing all they could to make him seem important, to make sure that his words and deeds would live on in people's minds. Without their efforts, who but a few cranks would still be talking about the miracle worker? The more they tried to wipe out the memory of him, the more vivid they made it. Did Haggai really think he could destroy an *idea* by such clumsy methods? He seemed too intelligent and calculating to make such a blunder. Then what was he attempting to do? Perhaps he simply wanted to efface the evidence of Jesus' power. If that was so, it was quite possible that he had been behind the murder attempt in Bethany. Perhaps, as pointed out by John, Haggai had been the first to wonder—because of the raising of Lazarus—if the Galilean really was the Messiah.

But Lazarus refused to act as "revealer"! He would not contribute to the fame of Jesus!

But if Haggai suspected, why had he let him go free? Why not keep him in prison forever, so that no one else could see him and start asking dangerous questions?

During the night, Lazarus tried to conjure up the darkness and solitude of his dungeon, but in vain. He wondered if it would have been better to remain locked up.

Next morning, he drew back as far as he could into the recess in the wall, and the Temple servants who came to clear the place for the last holy-water ceremony could not bring themselves to push him out with the rest.

Later, just before noon, as the high priest was filling the golden pitcher from the pool, Lazarus caught sight of Haggai, in his ceremonial garb, standing at the top of the steps with the other members of the Sanhedrin. He stared at him, willing the priest to look at him, and finally the priest did. More clearly than the day before, during the interrogation in the great audience chamber, Lazarus saw a strange fear in his eyes. A fear mixed with incredulity, as if Haggai did not want to admit that the man resurrected in Bethany was standing there, halfway between life and death, and watching him.

That's why he let me go, he thought. He's afraid of me. He has seen my wounds and he knows he is powerless against me.

When the procession moved away to the sound of lutes and cymbals, Lazarus felt like throwing himself at Haggai and demanding to know what he intended to do with Jair. But he would never have got past the guards stationed around the place.

He waited for the rest of the day, scrutinizing all the new arrivals at the pool, to see if Jair was among them. Why hold Jair prisoner? he thought. I should be the one shut up out of sight—not a beggar who looks like everyone else and whom no one would ever suspect of having been cured by a miracle.

Lazarus, who had always thought it ridiculous of Jair to make such a secret of going off every evening to some unspecified rendezvous, now realized that his friend had been right to be so careful.

In the evening, as the last songs of the Feast of Tabernacles floated down from the Temple, he thought about Susannah again: she had been with him last year in the Court of the Women for the final torch dance.

During the night he reproached himself for his sentimentality. Why did he need Jair? They never even spoke to each other! Was he incapable of being alone? Sooner or later he had better get used to it. Jair would not last forever, as he would. In his dungeon Lazarus had not complained of the lack of company! . . .

The next day, at the first hour, it started to rain, and most of the poor denizens left the pool and its narrow porticoes for the shelter of the city gates. Siloam was emptied of its beggars, the sick, the blind, the harelipped, and those missing an arm or a leg. Only two legless cripples and two paralytics lying on plank beds remained by the pool, not far from Lazarus, who gazed blankly at the little circles made by the rain in the rectangle of muddy water.

Jerusalem seemed strangely calm after the feast. The jumbled medley of music, singing, and prayer was replaced by the light patter of rain on paving stones. The lower city, emptied of its thousands of pilgrims, seemed deserted.

The lowering gray sky gave no indication of the passage of time. It might have been noon, or it might have been much later, when Jair appeared, drenched, and staggering, at the top of the steps. His face was white, as if he was in pain.

As soon as he saw him, Lazarus went to him and awkwardly put his weak arms out, to support him. Then he saw the blood on the back of the tunic, diluted by the rain.

"What did they do to you?" he cried.

"They gave me twenty strokes," Jair said faintly.

Clinging together in the rain, they slowly made their way to the recess in the wall. Once in its shelter, Jair slumped to the ground. Lazarus gently lifted Jair's tunic. From shoulders to hips, the skin of the back was raw, in shreds, a bleeding mass of straight deep cuts crisscrossed by purple welts. The Roman whip with the lead-trimmed thongs had been used.

175

"Why did you tell them the Galilean was the Messiah?" asked Lazarus in a low voice, so the cripples would not overhear. "Look what they've done to you!"

"I said nothing," replied Jair, "nothing! I didn't dare tell them what I believed. . . . I was afraid, because of the dark. I wanted to be let out. So I told them I didn't know if he was truly the Messiah. I said that I wasn't sure, that I had doubts, and that he was dead and I didn't care anymore."

"Why did they flog you, then?"

Jair did not answer.

"I'm a coward," he muttered finally. "I didn't deserve to be cured."

The occupants of Siloam had grown used to the strange companionship between Jair, the beggar, whom most of them had known when he was blind, and Lazarus, the man with the face of a corpse. But in the days that followed, they noticed a change in the two, though they still sat together in the same place, beyond the pool.

Before the arrest of the two by the Temple guards, the one they called the "dead man" was always silent. Now, he spoke, whereas the one who had been blind rarely did. The dead man, who never used to move, would now go up to the colonnades from time to time and beg, returning to share a bit of bread with his strangely stricken companion.

Twice a day, the dead man dressed the wounds on Jair's back. It was said that Jair had been flogged in a dungeon under the high priest's house. From a distance, the beggars watched the stiff bony fingers as they clumsily applied bandages made from strips of tunic.

176

Everyone believed that the two were close friends. Many would have liked to question the dead man, to find out who he was, where he came from, what ordeals he had been through, and what had happened to give him the face and body of a corpse, but the smell of damp earth that came from him kept them at a distance.

They noticed that Jair no longer went off every evening muffled in his cloak, with his face half hidden. He stayed, instead, in the recess by the pool with the dead man. Those who woke in the night often heard the two whispering, as if exchanging secrets. Jair seemed unable to sleep now, too. What had he done wrong, to be arrested and flogged like that? True, he had been different from the day his sight was restored by the false messiah, who wanted to destroy the Temple.

On moonlit nights, he was sometimes seen in a curious position, kneeling and with his eyes closed. A cripple lying near him once saw his lips moving, and on another occasion heard him praising Yahweh in strange terms.

But the other one, the dead man, never prayed.

Despite this difference, most of the destitute of Siloam agreed that these two shadowy creatures—thin, pitiable, indifferent to all that went on around them—got on perfectly well with each other.

Then came the month of Kislev, and the rain. The days grew chilly, the nights cold, and the beggars and cripples went to seek shelter under the colonnades of the Temple and in the caves in the area. They were so preoccupied with their own survival that they forgot the two strange companions by the Pool of Siloam.

Lazarus and Jair spent the first two months of the winter in one of the underground canals that had been blocked up and drained by the Romans years ago, when Pompey lay siege to Jerusalem. They knew no one would disturb them in that damp, cold, forgotten tunnel.

Lazarus would have liked to go farther in, to where there was no light at all, but for the sake of his companion, who could no longer bear the dark, he agreed to stay near the shaft of a well that opened to the surface just beyond Siloam and let in a little daylight.

And so, sometimes in silence, sometimes in conversation, they spent nearly all their hours underground, away from the rain and cold winds. Occasionally a bright sunbeam with swirling motes of dust would filter down to them. Then Jair would go and hold up his face to its light and warmth.

Lazarus, propped against the low curved wall, remained where he was. Not feeling the cold, he did not mind being ten cubits beneath the earth. Often he managed to drift into a pseudo sleep and would remember his own bottomless pit. Time no longer had meaning for him. Only the faint light from above reminded him of the alternation of day and night. He felt that he had been there for years, forever.

Every morning, as soon as the first glimmer of light came through the small opening, Jair, fighting down his fear of the dark, groped his way along the tunnel, which sloped gently upward, its ceiling becoming lower as it passed under the ramparts, until it emerged inside the city, near the Fountain of the Virgin. From there he would make his way to the courtyard of the Temple, or to the Pottery Gate on the other side of the city, to beg. Around noon he would return to Lazarus with water and a little bread.

He carefully avoided the district where Jacob and the others who had gathered to talk about the Galilean were hiding, and where Jair used to meet them before his arrest. He did not want to expose them to danger by going there, and, moreover, he felt unworthy.

But one morning the young man named Stephen came up and spoke to him as he was begging under the great arch of the Pottery Gate. "Why do you no longer come to see us?" he asked.

"Go away," said Jair, who had not seen him coming and therefore had been unable to avoid him. "You must not be seen with me."

But Stephen made light of the danger and sat beside him.

He told Jair that one of the scrolls containing John's writings had somehow fallen into the hands of the guards, so the scribes had to burn all the rest. "Luckily, we remember it all well enough to pass on Jesus' message by word of mouth."

And he described how some of them had taken to traveling the roads to spread the "good news."

"You're welcome to join us whenever you like," he told Jair as he rose to leave.

"But aren't you afraid of doing this in public?" Jair asked.

"What is there to be afraid of?" said Stephen.

That afternoon, Lazarus found his companion in a greater gloom than usual. But knowing that Jair was given to such moods after his shattering experience in the dungeon of the high priest, Lazarus asked no questions.

Ever since Lazarus revealed his story to Jair, little by little, day after day, in full detail, their relationship had changed. He was grateful to Jair for not insisting on how valuable this testimony might be, and for not urging him to carry out the "mission" entrusted to him by the Galilean.

And Lazarus had listened to Jair tell of his bewilderment and doubts, of the mental fog that made it impossible for him to understand anything, and of the way he despised himself for his betrayal during Haggai's interrogation.

So each unburdened himself to the other, and the other did not judge him. This brought to Lazarus a measure of peace at last. When Jair looked at him now, he saw a reviving flicker of life.

To protect himself from the cold, Jair wrapped himself at night in an old cloak he had bought for a few coins in the market. Although the wounds on his back were healed and no longer hurt, he had difficulty sleeping. He would lie for hours curled up on his side next to Lazarus, staring into the awful darkness, thinking of his fear and of the lie he had told the high priest. He could not forgive himself for his cowardice. But after his meeting with Stephen, he began to speak to Lazarus of his hope for a second chance, an opportunity, one day, to proclaim from the housetops that the Nazarene was the Messiah, the son of God, come to earth to replace the old Law with a new Law.

Lazarus listened and said nothing, no longer minding Jair's talk about the Galilean. Sometimes it seemed to him that his friend, without admitting it in so many words, longed for suffering and death.

When Jair did at last fall asleep, Lazarus, sitting propped against the wall beside him, would listen to him breathe. Remembering—each night—Susannah, he would rest his hand gently on his friend's cloak and let it rise and fall with the regular rhythm of the sleeper's breathing, as he used to long ago, in another world, when beneath his fingers he could feel the living warmth of his young wife's body.

Two weeks had passed since Jair's meeting with Stephen, and the *qadim* was blowing through Jerusalem, making sky and air crystal clear. Jair, freezing despite his cloak and the old rags tied around his legs and feet, begged under the arch of the Pottery Gate. There had been trouble between the Jews of Galilee and the Samaritans, and some, led by Eleazar, son of Dienus, and Alexander, had made up their minds to attack the inhabitants of Geman for killing a citizen of Jerusalem. So the Romans once again were checking everyone entering or leaving the city.

181

It was rumored that the previous day the magistrates and more than fifty members of the Sanhedrin, wearing *saq*s and with their heads covered with ashes, had gone to plead with the men getting ready to make war on the Samaritans, that they would only anger the Romans and bring down destruction on Jerusalem. Though many agreed that it wasn't worth risking the ruin of the country and the destruction of the Temple to avenge the death of one Galilean, the atmosphere was tense.

It was nearly noon. Jair, stiff in every limb, the skin of his face stinging in the icy wind from the east, noted ruefully that this unfrequented spot had yielded only one small bronze coin—not enough to buy even a bit of bread. He was about to set off for the market in the upper city, when he caught sight of a crowd at the end of the street. It was heading out of the city. He saw, in the lead, gleaming breastplates and gilded helmet spikes of Herod's guards. He could also hear shouts and the crack of a whip. Someone was being led to his death.

Roman soldiers hurried to the officer of the guards and brought the procession to a halt. Two priests in white head-dresses and a member of the Sanhedrin, recognizable by his long scarf, joined them, to confer. At last the centurion, though evidently dubious, ordered that the procession be allowed to continue.

Jair stood up to watch the prisoner stagger by. When he was no more than twenty paces away, Jair recognized him: it was Stephen they were dragging to the place of execution. Stephen could scarcely stand; his feet were bleeding from walking barefoot over the rough stones. His tunic was torn, revealing the lacerations on his body.

182

One of the guards tugged at his hair to make him walk faster. The crowd milled around him. Spectators came running from all directions. The guards, despite their spears, had difficulty restraining the mob in its eagerness for the coming spectacle.

Stephen was hit on the forehead by a sharp stone. He tottered, was grazed by another missile, and started to bleed from one cheek.

"Kill him!" shrieked a woman, while the Roman soldiers took positions along the ramparts, ready to intervene if the situation got out of hand.

Jair watched Stephen go by. The young man looked strangely calm. His face showed no fear.

The procession went through the gate, and Jair began to follow in the wake of the noisy crowd toward the Hill of Evil Counsel. They passed Gehenna, cleansed of its pestilential vapors by the wind, and finally reached the place of execution, where the prisoner was given a shove that sent him tumbling to the bottom of the dusty slope, among rocks dark with dried blood.

The spectators gathered around the edge of the crater, most of them picking up sharp stones to throw. The officer of the guards called for silence, and a member of the Sanhedrin read out the sentence.

"Stephen, son of Jeremiah, having uttered blasphemies against God and spoken publicly against the Holy Place and the Law, is sentenced to the death prescribed for infidels and agitators. Let his accuser cast the first stone."

An old man was led forward to the edge of the pit, and a stone was put in his hand.

Jair saw that Stephen, instead of crying out and trying to flee, as most victims did, got to his feet and stood quietly in the sunlight facing those who desired his death. He looked at the old man without hatred, without resentment, and did not even raise his arms to protect himself.

Taken aback, the old man turned around to ask what to do. A priest told him that, by the Law, since he was the first accuser, he must cast the first stone. Jair heard the old man quaver that he hadn't accused anyone.

"Yes, you did!" said a member of the Sanhedrin. "You told the guards who came to arrest him in the street that he said Jehovah wasn't to be found in the Temple, and you said the same thing again yesterday to the Council in the chamber of polished stones!"

The old man, terrified, looked at all the faces around him, faces distorted with impatience and blood lust. "But I didn't accuse him!" he wailed. "They told me to repeat what he'd said, and I did. That's all I did."

The crowd grumbled. "Hurry up, you old fool, if you don't want to go the same way as him!" someone yelled.

Jair, seeing Stephen stand there motionless and ready, felt a pang. He remembered his own cowardice after his arrest, when he had risked probably nothing worse than imprisonment in darkness. Stephen, impassive, almost smiling, had his head up and eyes wide open, seemingly unconcerned about the horror that awaited him.

Stephen had never been the subject of a miracle, and yet he would be the first to die for the Nazarene.

A scribe approached the old man, who still hesitated at the edge of the pit, and insisted that he obey the Law and cast his stone. The crowd grew more and more restive. The

Roman soldiers in the rear, their spears poised for action, were ordered to move five steps closer.

At last the old man raised his arm and threw the stone. But instead of hitting the prisoner, it rolled down the sandy slope and came to rest at Stephen's feet.

There was a howl from the crowd. "Let's start without him!" some yelled.

"Yes, get it over with! We've waited long enough! What a farce! The Romans will get fed up and send us home."

Then Jair spoke. "He's a good man," he said. "He doesn't deserve to die."

But his words were lost in the uproar.

Suddenly he felt like hurling himself into the pit with Stephen, there to stand up straight like him and defy these loathsome people. He went to the edge—but once again was paralyzed by fear.

The scribe picked up a heavier stone and put it in the old man's hand. But this time he held his arm, lifted it, and put his own strength behind the throw.

The stone hit Stephen on the brow. A roar came from a hundred throats, and a hail of stones followed. Stephen, still refusing to shield his face, fell on his side, blood streaming from his neck.

Jair turned and fled back to the city, his eyes brimming with tears.

When Jair returned to the Hezekiah Canal, he went and sat in the shadow, away from the well shaft. This was contrary to his custom, and Lazarus noticed that, equally strange, he had not brought back bread or water. Perhaps his friend could no longer endure their subterranean existence. But, not wanting to trouble him further, Lazarus refrained from asking questions.

They spent the afternoon sitting a few yards apart without exchanging a word.

At last, toward nightfall, when the faint light from outside began to fade, Lazarus went and sat beside his companion, who for all those hours had remained wrapped in his cloak, staring into the void. He asked Jair if he would like him to try to find something to eat before it was completely dark. Jair said he was not hungry.

For another long while they sat side by side. At last, very gently, Lazarus spoke.

"You must stop tormenting yourself like this. The Galilean never expected you to spend your life locked in the high priest's dungeon. That was not what he wanted of you, not why he gave you your sight. He never meant you to bear witness the way I was supposed to. You're lucky to see, to be alive. Your breath is warm, your body pulses with vitality. You shouldn't stay with me in this tunnel all the time. Go back into the sunlight. I'll understand. Just return at night, if you really want to. If you're always with me, who am half-dead, you'll never learn to take pleasure in anything again. Go to Keturah's place, or look for some other woman to give you back your hope and happiness.

"I'm not afraid of being alone—I must get used to it. . . . The best way to honor, to thank the one who made it possible for you to see the color of the sky at day and the myriad stars at night is to live out in the world, not beneath the ground like this."

"That's not the point," said Jair tonelessly.

"What is the point?"

"You wouldn't understand."

And again Jair withdrew into himself. Lazarus, for the first time since they moved into the Hezekiah Canal, realized that he would have to go up again, to the Pool of Siloam or somewhere else in Jerusalem, in order to release his companion from the darkness that was destroying him.

It was a long time, that night, before Jair's breathing became deep and regular. "I am dragging you down toward death," Lazarus whispered. His hand reached for the cloak over Jair's chest, then hesitated. Was not Lazarus only trying to steal some of the other man's life and warmth? Suddenly, he did not dare touch him.

Next day, as soon as the first faint gleam of dawn appeared at the bottom of the well, Jair awoke and left without saying a word.

This evening, we'll go back to Siloam, thought Lazarus, watching him disappear into the tunnel and the darkness that he so dreaded.

Haggai shrugged with annoyance when one of his servants came and told him that a beggar had been standing at the door of the house for hours asking to see him. He had had enough of the destitute coming to beg a few coins from him.

"Drive him off," he ordered.

"He claims you know him," answered the servant. "He says that his name is Jair, that he's the blind man of Siloam, and that he has important information for you."

Haggai sat up on his couch, surprised. What on earth could the wretch want? A flogging wasn't enough for him? . . .

"I know him," Haggai said.

Perhaps imprisonment and the rough treatment had finally made Jair see reason. Perhaps he had come to denounce some of his friends.

Haggai looked at the cup of curds and whey, the half-loaf, and the pot of honey untouched on the table before him. He could not make himself eat this morning. How would he get better if he didn't start taking some nourishment? He turned toward the inner courtyard. Rain had been falling steadily since the middle of the night.

Curiosity prompted him to see Jair, yet he was worn out, tired of hearing about the Messiah. It was too cold to listen to the ramblings of a liar and a fool. He glanced at the servant, who was awaiting his orders by the stove. . . .

But would it be right, given the exhausting struggle he had been engaged in for months—which would perhaps destroy him—to neglect even the smallest chance? No. The situation between the Romans and the Jews was too tense. The fight against these troublemakers must go on; it was necessary, now more than ever, to silence them.

"Very well," he said with a sigh. "Bring him to me."

Haggai stood up and went slowly around the balcony to the large room on the other side of the courtyard, where he received visitors. He wrapped himself in his cloak and sat stiffly on the divan facing the doorway.

When Jair was shown in, Haggai was astonished by his air of decision and self-confidence. The man planted himself in front of Haggai, head held high. The rain had drenched his tattered clothing and made the hair stick to his head. Large

188

drops ran down his face, which was paler and thinner than before. He looks like Lazarus, thought Haggai and shuddered.

Suddenly Haggai feared that Jair might have come to denounce his companion, the man from the grave—and Haggai never wanted *him* to cross his path again.

"I lied to you," said Jair, before Haggai could start to question him. "I believe Jesus of Nazareth was the Messiah, the son of the Most High. I testify that he came into the world to destroy and rebuild the Temple, to abolish the Law and replace it with another Law. I solemnly declare to you that he cured my blindness because he was the son of God. So that everyone may know it, I will proclaim this in the courtyard of the Temple and in all of Jerusalem."

Haggai, amazed, did not reply at once. He was relieved, however, that Jair's visit had nothing to do with Lazarus.

"Do you realize the seriousness of what you're saying?" he said at last. "You were flogged as a warning, and now you come and provoke me in my own house! Have you gone mad?"

"No," said Jair. "I truly believe he was the son of God— I am certain of it. I said nothing in the high priest's dungeon because I was afraid. But now my fear is gone."

Haggai slowly shook his head. If a wretch like this—no more than skin and bones, soaked, wearing rags—dared brave death for the Nazarene, then nothing could stop the disease from spreading. Haggai could picture a mob of beggars bursting into the hall of polished stones and bawling at the entire Sanhedrin that Jesus was the Messiah and they were ready to die for him.

"Do you know what happened yesterday to Stephen, son of Jeremiah, for saying what you have said?" he asked.

"Yes, I was there. Stephen was not afraid, either."

The rain was louder, and Haggai felt another dizzy spell coming on. He shut his eyes and held his breath, as he always did now to ward off the attacks. He had been having them since the Feast of Tabernacles, despite all the doctors' remedies. Why did he go on fighting it, his death? And not bow to the inevitable? He opened his eyes again. The beggar in his muddy cloak was staring at him.

"What do you want?" Haggai shouted. "Why do you come and tell me this, instead of proclaiming it to all the children of Israel, in the streets and markets of Jerusalem? What do you hope to get from me? A death like Stephen's? You can give up that idea. There won't be executions of that kind for a while now. No matter how much your friends get on the Romans' nerves, the procurator doesn't want more stonings in Judea. He wants order. We are forbidden to carry out our justice in public, while he can put up a hundred crosses every day outside the walls of Jerusalem. . . ."

"I do not seek death," said Jair. "I would rather live. But I'm not afraid anymore. That's all."

Haggai suddenly sensed a false note in Jair's confidence. When he looked closely, he could see that the man's hands were shaking. "Stupid," he murmured. "You are stupid."

What if I let him go? he thought. What if I say I am not interested? And that he can go and proclaim it to everyone in the Temple if he wants to? . . . The Romans would only arrest him in the end, and that would work against Israel. . . .

Jair still stood there facing him. What could have changed the beggar so, given him this courage, or recklessness? Once again Haggai had a vision of Lazarus. Perhaps *he* was behind this. Where had they been hiding all these weeks since their arrest? He noticed that Jair breathed with his mouth slightly open, and he thought he could hear that unbearable hoarse wheeze.

Haggai could swear he smelled rotting earth and rancid oils.

"What about your friend, the one who was raised from the dead—why isn't he with you today?" he asked. "Why hasn't he come, too, to proclaim that your Nazarene was the Messiah?"

"He's not a believer," Jair replied, lowering his eyes for the first time.

"Good for him," said Haggai. "Why can't you be as sensible?"

Jair lifted his head and smiled. He looked happy. For a moment, Haggai actually envied him.

The light, faint to begin with at the bottom of the well, gradually disappeared. When Lazarus noticed that it was getting dark, he was almost glad not to have Jair there beside him in the canal. It would do Jair good to stay away until morning; it might even give him back something of the life he was losing hold of day by day.

He waited until the darkness was total. Then, as he did every evening—usually without result—he tried to imagine himself suspended in another place, small yet limitless. Sitting still, he tried to forget the weight, even the very existence, of his body. His eyes were wide open, and soon it was as if the great sky stretched out above him, black as pitch. Concentrating on this immense, empty universe, so unlike the deep infinity of his own narrow pit, he finally saw again the single star he had seen at Tabgha, in the house of Simon, son of Zachariah.

The same speck of fire appeared in the east, in the midst of his darkness, and he had neither the time nor the strength to reject it. Then the huge man with red hair surged up in his memory; a threatening finger pointed; laughter resounded. Torches burned around him, and other faces appeared, filled with hatred, until more than ten men were lifting sticks to beat him, and a clenched fist materialized and struck him on the forehead, making a shower of stars explode before his eyes. Though he felt no pain, he flinched and drew his legs under him.

Why were the images of that horrible night coming back to him like this? He thought he had managed to repress them, along with other things from the past too painful, or too pleasant, to remember. He turned and put his cheek against the cold wall. He could not understand why sometimes, suddenly, he lost control of his memories like this. Perhaps these violent visions were somehow connected with Jair's absence. He shut his eyes and tried to feel his stiff, inert body floating in the narrow shaft of his tomb.

At last a numbness crept from his ankles to his knees and then his stomach. He breathed more slowly, and felt his neck droop. A mist veiled his mind, blurred his consciousness.

Soon there was a surprising sense of warmth, distant at first, then nearer and more distinct. There was a weight on his face. He seemed to have difficulty breathing, as if the air were congealing inside his chest. The black abyss over which he had only just started to float vanished. His eyes now were shrouded in white, and he could make out only vague areas of light and dark. Thick bandages pressed against his nose, his lips. His arms were tied to his sides, and his legs were bound together. He felt cold, colder than ever, and on his tongue, as stiff and hard as wood, there was the taste of earth. The heat on his face grew intense; his throat became unbearably dry. Then a force lifted him, dragged him up. He stumbled, as he had stumbled on the day he was raised from the tomb. . . .

Unable to endure this any longer, Lazarus stood, straightened as much as he could under the low roof, and moved toward the well shaft. He stayed for a while in the cool draft that blew from above. It was no use trying to lose himself in that false slumber. All it did was summon the cruelest images, the most painful memories.

Much later—exactly how much later, he couldn't tell—as he sat against the wall again, his mind free of tormenting images, he heard the scarcely perceptible sound of breathing close by. His first thought was of Susannah in their bed in the upper room. He restrained himself from going over to her and touching her bosom, warm through the fine linen of her shift. Then he remembered that he was alone in the Hezekiah Canal.

Listening, he again heard the sound of regular breathing, the breathing of someone asleep. His companion must have returned. He put his hand out toward the cloak over Jair's chest, but his fingers met only the clammy stones of the floor.

Four times Lazarus, alone in the canal, saw the light of morning filter down the well shaft. Four times he saw the light of evening fade. Jair now had been gone more than five days, and Lazarus began to worry.

He tried to persuade himself that Jair had taken his advice. That, more animated from having been in the streets of Jerusalem, or perhaps with his friend Keturah, Jair would soon be back with a little joy and hope in his heart. How easy it would be then for them to go back to Siloam, or somewhere else, inside or outside the city walls! They could go to another town, or to the uplands of Galilee, with its peaceful villages and hills dotted with trees. Once he had suggested to Jair that he might teach him the carpenter's trade, but there had been no response to that.

But would Jair agree to leave the holy city and get away from the constant danger, which seemed to hold a fascination for him since his arrest?

Outside, the sun was shining. The unusual brightness of the patch of light some thirty steps from where he sat signified the end of winter. But the thought came to him, a presentiment, that while he was safely hidden underground something terrible was happening. He kept seeing Jair's silent departure five days ago—Jair walking away, stooped, down the narrow passage and into the darkness.

During his sixth lonely night, while he was enjoying the sensation of floating in space in his bottomless pit, an unpleasant rubbing against his leg and ankle aroused him. Something was trying to drag him away by the foot. Then iron pincers tore at the rags around his feet, trying to rend the feeble flesh that they protected so poorly from the cold and damp.

He threw himself forward, struck at whatever it was that clung to him so fiercely. His fist encountered a warm mass,

194

rough hair. The creature sprang at him with a squeal, sinking its teeth deep in his face. Lazarus screamed and plucked at the animal biting his neck, throat, mouth. Before he could hurl it from him, the soft-bellied horror breathed into his mouth, and the warm gust filled him with nausea. Then he heard the thud of the thing's body hitting the wall, and he fled to the well shaft leading up into the night.

It took him a long time to master his fear, which reminded him, strangely, of what he had felt at Tabgha while hiding in the hills above Gennesaret to escape the man with red hair and his gang. A panic fear of death, a fear for his life— pointless and irrational.

It occurred to him later that the animal—a particularly large rat, probably starving—might just as easily have attacked Jair in his sleep and torn his face to shreds. Lazarus was none the worse for the attack, but what effect would it have had on his friend?

No, Jair must not spend one more day in this place of danger and death.

When he emerged from the canal after so many days underground, Lazarus was blinded by the light and could not keep his eyes open. Dizzy, he leaned against a wall. The heat of the sun on his brow and the mild breeze brushing his face told him that spring had come. It was a whole year since the Galilean had brought him out of his sleep, a year of undeserved punishment and purposeless suffering. The anger he had almost forgotten during his stay underground surfaced again, but he did his best to stifle it. All anger did was add to his misery.

Leaning on his staff, with the white light painful between his half-closed eyelids, he forced himself to walk to the Water Gate. He looked beyond the city, toward the Kidron valley, where there should now have been masses of flowers. But all he could see was a succession of neutral tones: the blue of the sky and the red of the earth and hills were lost to him. Just as on that far-off day on the roof of his house in Bethany, all he could make out was a wilderness of dim spaces and gray shapes. It was like being blind. For the first time, Lazarus understood the fear Jair must have felt in his dark dungeon.

All the shops in Jerusalem were closed, the doors shut. It was the Sabbath.

First he went to Siloam. At the foot of the steps were a few derelicts. Like him, they were returning from their winter quarters. Two paralytics lay on planks, and there was a blind man, and another with no legs, dumped like a parcel on the paving stones by the pool. But Lazarus saw no human shape in the recess in the wall. Jair, evidently, had not come back to Siloam.

Lazarus did not know where to look next. Where did Jair usually go to beg? . . . In the market of the lower city? But that would be closed on the Sabbath. The best place to pick up a few coins today would be the gates of the Temple or in the Temple courtyard.

Paying no attention to the Roman soldiers stationed on every street corner, he made his way along the Tyropoeon valley, through the poorest and dirtiest quarters of Jerusalem, to join the silent crowd of worshipers climbing the steps to the Royal Portico. A few ragged beggars stood with their hands outstretched at the entrance to the Temple. But Jair was not among them.

196

Lazarus went next to the white esplanade by the ritual baths. He looked for his friend under the arches of the Double and Triple Gates, but found there only a dozen people reminding the passers-by of their duty to give alms.

Continuing around the Temple, Lazarus reached the Golden Gate, which was also full of beggars, all unknown to him. Where could Jair be?

Jair might have left Jerusalem altogether and gone to one of the surrounding villages. Why not to Bethany, which Lazarus had so often talked about when they were in the canal?

As he approached the Sheep Gate, near the Antonia Fortress, he looked up and saw, through the mist still before his eyes and against the milky, dazzling expanse of the sky, hundreds of Roman soldiers with spears and shields lined up on the colonnades above the Temple courtyard. He remembered the things Jair had told him. Relations between Israel and the occupying power were worsening. Legionaries were stabbed to death in the streets. Ambushes, arrests, and crucifixions. Jair kept saying that the children of Israel should not fight the Romans—that the malady gnawing Israel came not from the infidels but from within.

Lazarus had sometimes suspected him of accepting, like many treacherous Sadducees, the presence of the enemy, of wanting to collaborate with them. He himself, a humble carpenter of Bethany, had never opposed the Romans and had paid his taxes regularly, though with reluctance. But he had always regarded their presence in his country as an insult to his people and to the religion of Israel. And he could not understand how Jair could so easily forget that it was the Romans who had crucified his messiah.

The faithful who entered the Temple looked somber on this

holy day that traditionally was celebrated with rejoicing. At the entrance to the court, silence reigned, not the usual music and singing. There were no crowds around the money-changers; every man, woman, and child stood motionless, bowed in prayer.

Despite his dimmed sight, Lazarus could see smoke rising over the sanctuary. So sacrifices were being offered up normally. There seemed no reason for the general dejection. But he had the feeling that something out of the ordinary was happening, that some tragedy was unfolding. He looked at the Jews around him. Their faces were tense, joyless. A few yards away, an old man wept.

Lazarus searched the whole court and went out by the last of the gates, the one opening on the upper city. Everywhere, even at the heart of the Temple, he encountered the same anxiety and sorrow. Alarmed now, he took the viaduct that led to the Hasmonaean Palace and, as he approached the wealthier quarters, became increasingly certain that at that very moment men were dying on crosses on Golgotha.

He found himself heading for the dreary streets by the Ephraim Gate, the alleys that led to the Hill of the Skull. When he reached the last stairway before the exit from the city, he remembered that it was from there, on the thirteenth day of the month of Nisan, just before Passover a year ago, that he had seen the Galilean, below, scarcely able to walk, his tunic torn, his arms tied to the beam that was to serve as the transverse part of his cross, and with a circlet of thorns on his head. Lazarus could almost hear the sound of the whip, could almost see the cripple striking the Galilean with his crutch and reviling him for not having cured him. And Lazarus remembered his own dismay and the question he had kept asking himself as he watched: How could a messiah, the saviour of Israel, passively accept so wretched a death?

The nearer he came to Golgotha, the more likely it seemed that an "agitator" like Jair, though not opposed to the Roman presence in Judea, could get himself arrested and condemned to death. The occupying power, exasperated by the outrages of the Zealots, was now unwilling to tolerate the least sign of trouble or unrest. As Jair had said, they were determined to preserve public order at all costs.

Lazarus stopped at the Ephraim Gate, afraid of what he might find beyond, on the accursed slope below the city walls.

A dozen legionaries were stationed outside, on the Jaffa road and by the path that led to the porticos on which the crosses were erected. As Lazarus had feared, several condemned men were dying, nailed hand and foot, on this Sabbath day. He imagined Jair's naked body limp and exhausted like the Galilean's, hanging from ropes around his arms and nails in his torn palms. Jair seems to have stopped breathing, his thin chest no longer rises and falls. Yet suddenly he braces himself on his feet and, with a supreme effort, manages to straighten up. He opens his eyes and rests them on Lazarus, who stands at the foot of the cross.

"Why do you leave me like this?" he seems to say. "Why don't you save me, you who cannot die and have nothing more to fear?"

Lazarus dismissed this horrible vision. He should go back to the canal and never come out again. If he did not learn the truth, he could go on thinking Jair was alive and happy in some unknown place far from Jerusalem.

But, instead, Lazarus stepped through the stone arch of the Ephraim Gate. At once he saw four wooden crosses, framed in the porticos, and four naked bodies roped and nailed to them. What remained of the mist before his eyes prevented him from distinguishing their faces. He started along the path to Golgotha, but a soldier ran up and barred the way with his spear.

"Where are you going?" he shouted.

"I want to see the condemned," said Lazarus.

The legionary, dumbfounded, stared, wondering where this character had sprung from. The ashen face, the cracked skin and unblinking eyes, the stinking rags—and the marks of two ugly bites, one black and still open above the gray lips and the other like a tear in rotten meat on the edge of the jaw. He looked at the thin legs and wondered how they had the strength to stand, much less walk.

"Not allowed!" he said. "Go back where you came from!"

Lazarus saw other soldiers approaching, spears at the ready. "At least tell me who they are," he implored.

"Murderers—that's who they are."

"Is one of them named Jair? Jair, the son of Joel?"

"I don't know," said the soldier. But as he turned to go, Lazarus clutched at him.

"Just tell me if Jair, the son of Joel, a beggar, is one of them! That's all I ask!" he cried.

Instead of answering, the Roman, revolted by the coldness of his touch and the stench that suddenly was overwhelming, gave Lazarus a shove that sent him sprawling in the dust.

Back at the Temple, Lazarus stopped every priest he met and asked where Haggai lived. The priests, scornful, disgusted, did not speak to him. It was not until nightfall, some

200

time after the hazzan had sounded the trumpet for the end of the Sabbath, that a Levite at last gave him the information he wanted: Haggai lived in an old house at the top of the street leading to Herod's Palace, in the Sion quarter, facing Mount Gareb.

Lazarus knew that if he went and knocked at the door, Haggai would refuse to see him, refuse to tell him whether or not Jair had been crucified. So he sat in a doorway opposite the house and waited all night without stirring, as he had waited once in a narrow street for John.

Throughout the night, he was plagued by the image of torn hands and a naked body falling into the mud. Toward the ninth hour he remembered that the Galilean had let out a long cry of pain and had tried to pull his hands free. Was it then that he had said something inaudible to one of the women in black at the foot of the cross, to Mary, his mother?

Lazarus feared that his companion had been crucified. In these empty hours of helplessness, it seemed to him that his own eternity would be like this endless night.

Purple gleams of dawn appeared over the tallest houses in the city. Not taking his eyes off the door, Lazarus saw several people emerge—servants, no doubt—and then a woman in a full red gown, whom he took to be Haggai's wife. Near the fourth hour, the wind started to blow, the sky became covered with thick gray clouds, and he could no longer see the position of the sun.

Sometime after midday, the heavy door opened again, and Haggai appeared at last, dressed in a black cloak, a turban, a kaffiyeh, and the long scarf of the members of the Sanhedrin. Without looking around, he went down the street that led to the Hasmonaean Palace and the Temple. He walked fast,

201

perhaps in a hurry to attend a meeting of the Council. Lazarus practically ran to overtake the priest and seized him by the arm.

Haggai swung around. "What do you want?" he cried, eyes wide, drawing away.

"Do you know where Jair is?" Lazarus asked. "I haven't seen him for seven days."

Haggai looked nervously at everything, at nothing. This agitation convinced Lazarus that the priest knew about Jair. He had been right to come to him.

"Was he one of those crucified on Golgotha yesterday?" he asked.

Haggai hesitated. He shifted his weight from one foot to the other.

"Answer me!" said Lazarus. "I must know."

"You should forget about him," said Haggai, still not facing Lazarus. "For your own good."

"I only want to know if he was on Golgotha."

"No," answered the priest. "He was not. . . . Now let me go. I have much to do."

As he turned away, Lazarus touched him again, and again saw terror in his face. He realized that this powerful man was afraid of him.

"If he didn't die on the cross, where is he? Did you put him in prison?"

"Your friend Jair was a fanatic," Haggai said. "Imprisoning him, flogging him again, would have been pointless."

"What have you done with him, then?" cried Lazarus, catching him by the arm once more. The priest shrank, chilled, from this living corpse. Lazarus, aware of the power he had over him, held on more tightly. "Where is Jair?" he repeated. "I won't let you go until you tell me."

At last the priest looked him in the face. "Go!" he said. "I'm ill, and all this talk about messiahs doesn't interest me anymore."

"Where is he?"

Haggai shook his head slowly, but did not answer. Then, with a smile that was a grimace, he spoke: "You claim, I believe, that there is no such thing as death, that it's only an emptiness, a black abyss. . . . Isn't that what you told me when I came to see you in Bethany a year ago? You also said, if my memory serves me, that death is a thousand times better than life. That's what you said in Caiaphas's house— your exact words. And I'm quite willing to believe you speak from experience. . . ."

He paused. Lazarus gripped his arm more tightly.

"So you can be glad," the priest went on. "Your friend now enjoys the happiness that has been denied you. It may even be that where he is now, in that black abyss of yours, he is happier than he ever was on earth. The man, after all, led a wretched life. . . . His desire for death, perhaps it came from listening to you and not, as one might think, from his confused religious beliefs. He was weak, easily influenced. He asked nothing more than to believe. . . . And you gave him something to believe."

There was silence. Lazarus stared at Haggai, stupefied. Their faces almost touched.

"When did it happen?" he asked at last.

"On the eve of the Sabbath. Since he couldn't be executed publicly, he was beheaded in his cell. . . . He provoked us, and there were only two votes in his favor in the Sanhedrin. The old quarrels about your Messiah no longer exist among us. Pharisees and Sadducees are of one mind. Danger has brought us together . . . for the time being."

The priest looked suddenly weary. Lazarus, still stunned by what he had heard, let go of his arm.

"I agreed with the sentence," said Haggai, "even though I knew it was pointless."

Released, Haggai walked away. But after a few yards, he turned. "Leave Jerusalem," he said. "There is nothing but suffering for you here."

Thinking all this must be a waking nightmare, Lazarus went down again to the lower city. Paying no attention to the bustle in the narrow streets, the shouts of the vendors, the pushing and shoving of the crowd, he left Jerusalem by the Water Gate and went in the direction of the Kidron valley, leaning on his staff.

Wandering like a sleepwalker, he found himself in the old cemetery of Jerusalem, among the "graves of the judges," where, according to the Scriptures, the trumpets of the Last Judgment would sound. He stood in the midst of monumental sepulchers, their pillars and pediments arranged in a circle like the walls of a crater. He looked at Absalom's urn, and thought of all the dead around him: the kings and priests, the daughter of a pharaoh buried there long ago, in the days of the kings of Judah. . . . Would he, like them, one day find peace? Would the last trump sound for him, too? Would there be an end to his eternity? And then—would he become one of the multitude who rose from the dead? Or would he be the last alive, the one man remaining in a world of fire and burning embers?

He sat on a flat stone facing the walls of the city. His mind a blank, he stared a long time at the tomb of Joab the high priest. When he came to himself, the moon, white as a ghost, was flooding the sky. Gazing at the horizon, he saw a mountain of skulls. Around him were the twisted black skeletons of cedar trees and the pale shapes of pillars, pyramids, pediments, and urns.

He saw the shining blade of a sword fall suddenly, and Jair's head drop in a shower of blood to the earthen floor. . . . What had they done with his friend's remains? Thrown them to the dogs, or left them to rot in the well under Caiaphas's house?

He saw yellow resin torches along the ramparts. The Romans were watching the city more closely than ever, ready to pounce at the first sign of unrest. Behind those closed walls and crenelated towers, people slept. How many remembered the Galilean crucified a year ago on Golgotha? How many knew that a blind man, miraculously cured, a mere beggar, had died nearby, only yesterday, because of that same false messiah? . . . Indifferent, they lay deep in sleep. The stories of visionaries and fanatics did not matter to them.

For years he, too, had slept like that, not bothered by the folly or the misfortune of others.

To hear Jair breathing beside him, to put his hand on his chest and feel its regular, peaceful rise and fall!

Lazarus looked up. The sky was very bright. White light shone on Jerusalem, on its high colorless walls bristling with uneven, square towers. The holy city might disappear, the Temple might be razed by the Romans—it would not matter to him. He remembered the fear on Haggai's face. Then chaotic images rose before him: the leering face of the man with red hair; the torn palms and the naked body in the mud; Susannah's face bending over him, her astonishingly fair neck; Jair stooping as he disappeared down the dark tunnel of Hezekiah.

Had he not sensed, that last morning, that his friend had decided to die? Yet he had done nothing to stop him!

And perhaps he had indeed helped drive Jair to that extremity. How many times had he said that death was nothing, that death was better than a miserable half-life? Haggai was right to say he was responsible. He had thoughtlessly made death lose its terrors for Jair. By talking about it with such longing, he had made it familiar to him, almost desirable.

Lazarus got up and walked through the night. He stopped on the slope of Mount Scopus, above the Temple and the Antonia Fortress, which were lighted by a hundred torches. There, wanting to weep but unable to shed a tear, he stood waiting for daybreak.

At dawn the first thing he saw was the flat desert to the south, barren, empty, strewn with white stones.

FOUR

After Jair's death, Lazarus, now always alone, heard no news but what he was told occasionally by the derelicts at Siloam.

Thus he learned of the death of Tiberius, that Tiberius's successor was the emperor Caligula, only twenty-four years old. Lazarus lived, indifferent, through the troubles resulting from the Jews' refusal to worship the new master of Rome and the punishment this brought down on them.

The excitement caused by the Galilean's miracles and teachings seemed long forgotten. During the summer following Jair's death, a few strangers came, one by one, to see Lazarus at Siloam, but after that no one bothered him about the miracle of his resurrection, which he obstinately refused to talk about.

For him, huddled in his recess in the wall, the days and the years went by slowly. Light alternated with dark, sun with rain. More dead now than alive; free at last, after many struggles, of memories and thoughts; rid even of the remorse that had plagued him for years over Jair's tragic end, Lazarus no longer rebelled, no longer questioned. He had stopped suffering.

A rumor was heard at the Pool of Siloam that Caligula had gone mad and been murdered in his own palace, that the new emperor was Claudius, who stammered. Then it was said that a new king, Agrippa, ruled Judea, by arrangement with Rome, and was persecuting those who still dared to speak in the name of Jesus of Nazareth. It was said that Peter, a disciple of the Galilean, had been arrested, and that the high priest, taking advantage of the short interval between pro-curators, and in defiance of Roman regulations forbidding the Jews to carry out their own public executions, had had a man named James stoned to death outside the city walls.

Lazarus was indifferent to all this, as he was to his own fate.

Other summers, other winters passed, until one day, during the Feast of Tabernacles, an unforeseen event brought him face to face with reality again, reviving all his former pain.

For years the Temple servants had refrained from turning the "living corpse" out of the Pool of Siloam along with the rest of the destitute before the holy-water ceremony. As if unaware of his presence in the recess of the wall. So on that festival morning, as the high priest, clad in his ceremonial vestments—the headdress swathed in blue cloth, the tunic, surplice, chasuble embroidered with crimson and gold thread, the pectoral studded with precious stones—knelt at the foot of the steps and filled the pitcher before the assembled crowd, the members of the Sanhedrin, and representatives of the twenty-four orders of the clergy, Lazarus, hidden in the shadows, was free to look at the spectators standing around the pool.

As he idly scanned a group of pilgrims, something inside him, indefinable, told him that there was a familiar face among the men and women on the roof of a nearby house. A forgotten feeling of curiosity and excitement made him concentrate. One by one, he scrutinized the faces as they watched the high priest. Soon, in the sixth person along the edge of the roof, despite the white beard and wrinkled forehead, he recognized Eliphas, his apprentice. On his ear Eliphas wore the wood chip that denoted a carpenter. Beside him was . . . a woman. For a brief moment, Lazarus felt like turning away or hiding his face in his hands. But he could not.

At first he refused to admit that this stout old woman, with her busy gray hair, her little deep-set eyes and shrunken lips, could be Susannah, his young wife. He stared at her. She looked serious, intent on the ceremony taking place below. Her fleshy cheeks were no longer reddened with *sikra*, her graying eyebrows and dull eyes no longer enhanced with blue-black kohl. Her chin was heavy; her bead necklace seemed to make her wrinkled neck sink further between her shoulders; her tight belt only made her waist look thicker. . . .

A thousand long-suppressesd images rose in Lazarus's memory. A girl of thirteen with a full red mouth like an anemone, cheeks pink as the flesh of a pomegranate. The same woman, still a child, when he went, in his best clothes, to fetch her from her father's house, across a distance that was all time and space, to his own house on the other side of Bethany. . . . A bright face bending over him, a supple, dazzling neck that swelled, stretched, arched. Curly black hair falling to smooth bare shoulders. A childish hand, with stubby, caressing fingers and transparent blue-veined skin. A row of young teeth. A burning breast, golden as honey, and curving hips, and parted legs. Long sighs, quickening breath, tenderness, desire, and entering slowly her warmth. . . .

After all those years in the recess in the wall, Lazarus left the Pool of Siloam soon after the Feast of Tabernacles. He did not have the courage to remain in a place where he would be forever haunted by the picture of Susannah so sadly aged and faded, and by the memory of Jair, his departed friend.

He made for the country north of Jerusalem, leaving the city through the Dolorosa Gate, near the Antonia Fortress. Although his first thought was to disappear into the desert, he stopped by the road to Caesarea, at one of the construction sites started by King Agrippa some years before. It was supposed to have been a new city wall, but the work was discontinued by order of the Romans. Lazarus installed himself in a cavity at the foot of the wall, surrounded by abandoned building materials, broken planks, split beams, and large blocks of stone that had never been used. He spent part of the winter hidden there, outside the city but not more than a hundred steps from the Temple.

Seeing Susannah, now an old woman, had made him realize how terrible was his loss. His days and nights had been alike;

he had not noticed the passing of the weeks or years, had not suspected how much time had elapsed since he left his tomb—never thinking of Susannah with a face and body other than the face and body she had the day he left her. It did not occur to him that she might change.

Until he saw her with his own eyes—heavier, wrinkled—he had entertained a hope, an unconscious hope, of another miracle, despite his refusal to accept the Galilean as the Messiah. Had he not been brought back from the Great Sleep? Compared to that, the recovery of his strength would be nothing. But there was no point now in nourishing that vague hope.

Curled up in his hiding place, lying on the half-frozen ground between blocks of stone, with the cold winter sun searing his eyes, he decided that it would be best to take refuge in darkness. Then, at least, he would not see the flowers spreading over the hills in spring, the trees, the city walls, the smoke rising over the Temple. He would not have to watch pilgrims and merchants coming and going on the road to Caesarea. He would not hear the hazzan sounding the trumpet in the evening, or the praying and chanting floating across every day from the Court of the Priests. The only way to forget all these unbearable manifestations of life was to return to the Hezekiah Canal.

The thought of the animal that had attacked him there still filled him with the utmost repugnance, but he reasoned that he would be safe from bites if his face, neck, and hands were covered with rags. So one morning he went and begged in the Royal Portico at the entrance to the Temple, in order to get enough money to buy an old tunic or a piece of blanket to tear up for that purpose.

In a week he had collected what he needed, and went to the market in the lower city. Crossing Jerusalem, he found that many shops were shut—empty, apparently looted, sometimes gutted by fire. Many houses, too, were abandoned. Some of the doors bore the sign the Romans made to indicate that the former occupants had been imprisoned, deported, or crucified. Wherever he went, he saw armed soldiers, on every flight of steps, on every street corner. It was as though two more legions had been stationed in Jerusalem. The market, usually so busy, was half empty. Lazarus concluded that the Jews were hiding in their houses.

He overheard three men talking, almost in a whisper, about new violence that had broken out between Judea and Samaria. He did not listen. It did not concern him.

He wandered through branches of the canal. Bent double, sometimes almost crawling through pools of stagnant water and black mud, groping in the darkness with his hands and feet protected by strips of tunic tied together, he explored the whole network of abandoned passages. At last he stopped in a cul-de-sac far from any opening or ray of light. To avoid being bitten, he wrapped his face and neck in pieces of old clothes he had bought for that purpose. Then he sat with his back against the wall and drew his knees up to his chin.

He soon saw that although it was darker and more silent here, in this veritable tomb, than at Siloam or by Agrippa's wall, he still could not shake off thoughts of the past. On the contrary, his memory seemed more vivid than ever, and he had to struggle with it once again.

All the events of his life, the most trivial and the most important, unfolded before him. It would have been a consolation, if living everything over again at least helped him understand why this punishment had befallen him. But, instead, the endless procession of scenes only bewildered him more.

He had never disobeyed the Law. His only sin—his responsibility for Jair's death—had occurred too late to explain his fate. He could find nothing reprehensible in his past.

As a child, he had studied the Law diligently in the synagogue; had praised God morning and evening in his own words; had always honored his father and mother. When he was thirteen, the age of assuming a man's duties, he began to recite the Shema three times a day, and he fasted on all the prescribed days and the Day of Atonement. He entered the Temple through the Court of the Men. On his bar mitzvah, he was proclaimed a son of the Law, and read from the Scriptures in public. Then he began to work in his father's shop, to learn the honorable trade of a carpenter. Soon he could trim wood skillfully. He made his first chest and table with his own hands. His beard started to grow, and he began to groom himself and perfume his hair. He decided to look for a wife.

At nineteen, before he was married, he closed his dead father's eyes. A few months later, he performed the same office for his mother. He anointed them with oils and sweet herbs, and buried them with much lamentation.

He honored the Almighty every day of his life. Never coveting the possessions of others, never lusting after another man's wife. He worked from sunrise to sunset to give his wife and sisters a decent life and protect them from want. He always gave to the poor and helped those in distress—like the Galilean carpenter who knocked at his door one autumn night seeking shelter from his enemies.

He could remember that accursed night perfectly, better than any other. John sat silent at the table, and, opposite him, the big man with the goatee, who jumped up nervously at every sound. And the Galilean, his hair dusty and his tunic made of two different pieces of cloth, talked at length in a slightly ludicrous accent, claiming he was the "light of the world" and that whoever followed him "would not abide in darkness."

Lazarus had shared his bread with them, his wine and dried fish. For them, he had not hesitated to risk danger.

And to thank him for his hospitality and protection, the Galilean had condemned him to this eternal torment worse than *sheol*!

What would have happened if, instead of scrupulously obeying Yahweh's Law that evening, Lazarus had left the false messiah out in the street, at the mercy of his enemies? Might not Lazarus now be suspended peacefully in the bottomless pit?

Sometimes he had the terrifying thought that he was doomed to rot, half-alive, forever, because Yahweh did not exist, and never had existed. And that everything the children of Israel had put their faith in, that he had put his faith in, was a lie.

Lazarus, sitting in his courtyard by the open door of his workshop, sensed someone behind him. Turning, he saw Nathan in the doorway. Nathan had on his best tunic, embroidered, with ornamental colored strips and a sash of woven silk. The smell of marjoram came to Lazarus from the young man's clean, strong body; Nathan had anointed himself for the Sabbath. Lazarus looked at him closely: he was getting more and more like his mother. The same full lips. And the eyes, though blue, a rarity in Judea, were just as bright as hers. The boy, seventeen, was now a head taller than Lazarus.

Old enough, thought Lazarus sadly, to be looking for a wife and leaving home. Wistfully he recalled the time when he could hear Nathan playing in the courtyard under the window of his workshop.

"I finished Judah's chest," Nathan announced with pride.

"Good," said Lazarus. "We'll tell him tomorrow in the synagogue, and Sunday he can come and fetch it."

He looked at his son again. He loved his high forehead and determined jaw. A shame, that the boy had not let his beard grow. Lazarus hated the fashion of clean-shaven faces and short hair; they made the Jews look like heathens. Nathan, uncomfortable under his father's scrutiny, went back into the workshop, leaving Lazarus alone in the courtyard.

Lazarus looked at his strong carpenter's hands. They were becoming gnarled and twisted. Blue veins stood out against the weathered skin, which was marked by lighter traces of old wounds, long since healed. Only the cut he had given himself with his knife two days ago was still a little red and swollen. He remembered what his fingers were like when he was Nathan's age—long and slender, almost feminine. . . . He shook his head, thinking of the years that had passed so quickly.

The village street stretched out in front of him between the square, white, flat-roofed houses like his own. The hill, it being early spring, was covered with yellow crocuses and patches of pink almond blossom. The sun was setting behind the olive grove, and long shadows crept over the red earth. Lazarus could hear the sound of children playing, and the voice of his sister Martha in the upper room. He thought of Isaiah's table, which had to be ready as soon as possible, and the beams Eliphas must finish trimming for Thomas. . . .

Orders were coming in faster than ever, but this evening he felt tired. His back was stiff: he had been planing all afternoon, bent over his bench. Where was the stamina he used to have? He gazed around the courtyard, and it seemed to him that everything was aging, even the stones on the ground. With time, all things wore out. Looking up at the darkening sky, he saw the first star. Even the stars were born, grew, shone, and then faded. He had observed that some became paler every night, until they vanished forever.

When the hazzan's trumpet sounded three times from the highest roof in Bethany to announce that the Sabbath had "started to shine," Lazarus went inside. The lamps were lighted in the large room that served for cooking and eating. His wife and sister had set the table with dates, figs, wine, bread, and herbs. Nathan and the two women were waiting for him, reclining on the couches. Susannah, wearing her fine linen dress, had braided her hair with colored ribbons and reddened her cheeks with *sikra*. As he came nearer, he saw that she had put on her old round earrings, gold as the sun, his first present to her before they were married. Martha, over forty now, was an old woman beside her. Time seemed to have no power over Susannah; it passed without touching her. Lazarus looked at her full red lips, her bright eyes, her slim waist, and told himself that he was a happy man. Sitting down quietly beside her, he began to recite the Triple Blessing.

As he bent in prayer over the sanctified food—the full pitcher, the bread, the fruit—he heard shouting, muffled and distant, over his head. He bowed lower. Then a blow shook the walls around him. It was followed by another. . . . He stopped praying and bit his lip. He could feel water rising to his ankles. He sat up, looked around wildly. He must not yield, he must not give up. Everything had been going so well, before . . . when nothing broke the silence!

For an instant he was alone in the dark. Then the pale

patch that was Susannah's still-youthful face reappeared.
. . . She was there beside him, her head bowed in prayer.

Lazarus hurried down the straight main street of Bethany.
All night the blows shook the ceiling and walls. A hundred
times he had thought he would lose Susannah, asleep at his
side on the bed in the upper room. His stomach tightened
with fear as he made his way to the other end of the village,
to the synagogue on the hill by the river.

This morning he had draped his white silk tallith over his
head and shoulders, and now he was on his way to the Sabbath
service, accompanied by Nathan and Joshua, Mary's husband, and followed by Susannah and his sisters.

Going up the steps and through the antechamber used as
a schoolroom, he entered the synagogue, which was already
crowded. It was a large rectangular room divided into three
sections by lines of pillars that supported the women's gallery.
He greeted the men of Bethany, also in their prayer shawls,
and parted from his son and brother-in-law to take his place,
the best, in the front row, facing the ark. The place had been
accorded him in recognition of his virtues over the years. He
could smell the fresh scent of the mint water sprinkled on
the floor before the service to purify the air, and he thanked
the Almighty silently for the health and happiness that had
been granted him.

Then Ephraim came forward. Standing on the dais in
front of the ark, his arms outspread, he began to recite the
Shema:

Hear, O Israel: The Lord our God is One.

And everyone turned toward the Temple in Jerusalem and answered loudly:

Blessed be the Name of His kingdom forever.

But Lazarus heard shouts and a hundred rushing footsteps overhead. Despite his desire to honor God with those around him, he could not help remembering his gloomy thoughts of the day before: how time passed inexorably, how Nathan would soon leave him, how the stars, too, grew old and dim.

Looking up, he saw Eliphas in the second row, beside the dais, his beard turned white, and Samuel, his father's friend, now a helpless old man. Also Simon and Eleazar, with whom he had played as a child, and Judah, whom he had held in his arms when he was less than a year old, and who was now waiting for the chest Nathan had just finished for Miriam, his wife, for her dresses and shawls. . . .

The ground shook under his feet again, but he gathered his strength to pray with the others.

And thou shalt love the Lord thy God
with all thy heart and soul and might. . . .

Praising Yahweh, they did not hear the noise overhead. Lazarus wanted to join in, but he found he could not move his lips. He was losing his grip again on these images. Through a thin mist he saw Rabbi Jehuda holding the scrolls of the Law. The water, which had been rising slowly, reached his

221

ankles. Lazarus turned to look for his son in the fourth row, but the faces there were only blurs.

Opening his eyes, he saw Susannah coming to lie beside him on the bed. The lamps were lighted in the upper room; it was evening.

He put his hand gently on her gray hair, touched the wrinkles in her brow. Felt her sunken lips, her missing teeth. He was filled with an inexpressible tenderness. "We've grown old together," he said. "How many times has the sun risen since the blessed morning I fetched you from your father's house?"

"True," answered Susannah. "The years have passed, my beloved, and the happiness we shared has kept us from seeing our lives ebb away. The olive tree we planted on the hill the day after our wedding has grown to be as tall as the rest, with a trunk more gnarled each year. How many times have we gathered its fruit for the Feast of Tabernacles?"

Slowly, he caressed her, then rested his head on her heavy bosom. His cheek could feel the warmth of her skin, still soft and smooth. She stroked his forehead, ran her fingers through the hair he still had, and he told himself again how happy, peaceful, and pleasant his life with her had been.

He sat up and embraced her, put his mouth on hers, and felt desire rising within him as it had long ago. When he was with her, he was not afraid of death.

But there was a sudden crack overhead, and daylight flooded in through a wide cleft. The water in the canal reached his knees.

222

Lazarus struggled through the tunnel. The rising water, now at his waist, slowed his progress. The wall that Pompey had built to block the supply channels must have collapsed. Blinded by the light from above, he tore off the rags that had protected his face and hands for so long from the bites of rats. . . .

What was happening? He did not need this . . . he needed Susannah, Nathan! Reality must not be allowed to destroy the world he had constructed so patiently, so carefully, and with such difficulty.

The floor and walls of his underground refuge trembled. Dreadful things must be going on in Jerusalem, events that might threaten his own false happiness, the fruits of his imagination as dear to him, almost, as his vision of the bottomless pit.

The water continued to rise. Soon it was up to his chest and made walking almost impossible. He could not remember the way to the exit under the ramparts. Would he fall into some hole in the bed of the canal? But what would that matter, since he could not drown? . . . Still, he was afraid.

Finding himself in darkness again, in a place where the ceiling had not given way, he turned back toward the dazzling light. The water, pulled by a strong current toward the deepest channels, seethed around him. It was difficult now to remain upright.

There was another loud crack, and a stone fell on his shoulder. He barely had time to flatten himself against the wall before the whole roof collapsed. In the uproar that followed, the water came up to his face. He felt himself losing his footing, being carried away, unable to breathe. He struggled, but found no footing, no bottom, in the torrent. More stones fell, their impact hardly cushioned by the water. Stunned, he became helpless, limp, and was swept away. His throat and lungs filled with water, and as he sank, half conscious, he had a brief vision of the narrow walls of his tomb.

Then his head emerged from the water, into the open air, under a blinding sun. He tried to drag himself out onto a heap of stones. Twice he fell back. He twisted his ankles and skinned his hands, but at last pulled himself to dry ground, where he lay, exhausted, in the debris of a collapsed wall.

He lay on his side, one hand over his eyes, not understanding what was happening. There was a warm breeze on his face, so it had to be summer. But Jerusalem was strangely silent. As if there had been some terrible disaster.

Not wanting to know, he forced himself to think of the false happiness he had left behind in the canal: of Susannah, young despite the passage of time, with her narrow waist and full red lips; of his sister Martha, now an old woman; of his son, and the blue eyes that were so rare in Judea. . . .

The sound of a child crying in the distance made him open his eyes. At first he could not believe what he saw. The ramparts by the Fountain Gate had been torn apart. The ropes, massive hide-covered shaft, and heavy iron tip of a Roman battering ram jutted from the rubble. The tower of Siloam had been knocked down, too. All that was left was a fragment of wall pointing up to the sky. Around the pool, a few houses were still burning. Dozens of bodies, of men, women, and children, lay with their throats cut in the half-dried-up bed of the Tyropoeon river, whose thin trickle of water was red with blood. Nearby, a swarm of black flies buzzed over the open belly of a little girl still clutching her wooden doll. The ground was strewn with the corpses of both Jews and Romans. In the middle of a deserted street three starving dogs fought over the remains of a carcass dragged from the ashes of a house.

Lazarus sat, incredulous. Farther off, beyond the ruins of the lower city, the ruins of the Hasmonaean Palace could be seen through the swirls of black smoke that hung over everything. But it seemed that the Temple, not far from the palace, was still intact.

So had it been the sounds of war he had heard in the canal? Could the Jews and the Romans have massacred one another?

Suddenly thinking of Susannah and Nathan, he climbed up to the broken ramparts, over the rubble, and looked toward the hill. Beyond the long line of forts that had been built around the city to lay siege to it, he saw the fire that was consuming what remained of Bethany.

He went through the streets of the lower city toward the Temple, apparently the only structure left standing.

On the way, he saw shattered monuments, burned houses, looted shops, and dead Jews and Romans lying in their mingled blood. In the Fountain quarter, he stopped by the corpse of a girl no older than Susannah had been on their wedding day. She was dark and wore a blue dress. Her hair was braided, her lips were still red, and as she lay on the pavement, her eyes stared up, unseeing, at the sky. There was no sign of injury; one might have thought her still alive. Lazarus gazed for some time at the white face, frozen yet still beautiful, and wished with all his heart that he had not survived the flood in the canal.

He hobbled on. The farther he went through this dreadful scene, sometimes having to climb over still-smoking ruins, the more surprised he was not to encounter a single Roman or one of the city's defenders. Were there no survivors? Where were the legionaries and their army of looters and murderers hiding? Listening carefully, he heard a faint noise, and looking toward the Temple, saw a thin column of smoke starting to rise over the colonnades facing the Antonia Fortress. Was there still fighting around the sanctuary?

As he approached the Temple, he saw a group of rebels at the end of the street. They were crowded around the foot of the steps leading from the Tyropoeon valley up to the Court of the Gentiles. He could not run, and had no staff to lean on, but he somehow managed to catch up with them before they entered the Temple.

He was the last one through the Royal Portico, and, once inside, a dozen men, sword in hand, shut the heavy bronze doors behind him.

He was stunned by what he saw. Thousands of people were gathered within these impregnable walls. The air was filled with the sound of flutes and tabors. As smoke from a sacrifice rose, most of the Jews prayed, palms upward, heads bowed. Each had a dagger at his side and a tallith over his head and shoulders. They praised the Almighty, who "would never allow his house to be destroyed." Looking up, Lazarus saw that the colonnades were lined with defenders, and that square wooden towers had been built at the corners and on the highest point. One of these was on fire. Lazarus concluded that there must still be fierce fighting going on by the ditches at the foot of the walls.

Everyone in the crowd was gaunt, skeletal. Jerusalem must

226

have been through a long siege. Many were too ill or weak to stand, and prayed as they lay on the ground. But even in their eyes, though some were near their end, shone the light of a faith stronger than death.

Lazarus felt close to them. Although he belonged to no people or nation now, he was proud of their serenity, their confidence, and their great courage.

The noise he had heard from the lower city was coming from the other end of the esplanade, hidden from him by the sanctuary wall. He hesitated whether to investigate. The fighting seemed to be by the Sheep Gate, and he was not sure he wanted to see for himself the danger threatening the heart of Jerusalem. It was said that the Jews, shut up like this in the Court of the Gentiles, had held out three months against Pompey's army. But enduring a siege was one thing, repelling an invader another. Pompey had finally entered the Holy of Holies in triumph, "out of curiosity." Would another Roman general dare repeat that sacrilege today?

Passing the Beautiful Gate at the northwest corner of the esplanade, Lazarus could see that the high walls and four towers of the Antonia Fortress had been razed. He stopped.

Battering rams and other heavy war machines had already breached the defenses of the Temple, and the Romans were using the rubble to complete a ramp they had built over the moat and the Pool of Struthion. The soldiers, despite missiles of all kinds raining down on them, had almost finished clearing a way in. Behind them, cohorts were assembling, in impeccable order, ready to enter in force.

There was no hope. Before the sun went down, the Temple itself would be destroyed—burned, razed.

Of Jerusalem, of Israel, nothing would be left.

Lazarus shut his eyes. What foolishness could have brought things to such a pass?

Was it to witness this catastrophe that he had been snatched from the darkness of his canal, from his other life, so peaceful and pleasant compared with this?

Hymns to the glory of God were being sung on all sides, and sacrificial smoke still rose, while many men, forgetting their weaknesses, were taking their swords in their hands and getting ready to fight.

This Temple had once been his, too. Why could he not join in its defense and die, with the others, for its sake?

A new sound came up from the ramp, and he felt a pang in his chest. He had a vision of Susannah's smooth young face and parted red lips, but he banished it. Susannah was dead. She had turned into an old woman with no lips, a heavy bosom, and gray hair, and then she had died. For years now she had been lying in her tomb in Bethany, like his beloved sisters, Martha and Mary. There was no point in thinking about them or about Nathan.

He shook his head. Why had he been afraid, a few hours ago in the canal, when the current swept him away? Had he not caught a brief glimpse of his bottomless pit as the water filled his throat and lungs? . . . What had he been trying to save when he struggled against that?

What was he still afraid of?

He remembered Jair, bent over, disappearing one morning down the tunnel in the Hezekiah Canal. No one was more afraid of death, and yet, that day, he had gone willingly to meet it.

Lazarus opened his eyes again. Some of the women and children were taking refuge in the sanctuary. The rebels were

228

forming into three ranks to confront the Romans. Sword blades flashed in the sun.

Suddenly the vision returned, long forgotten, of the torn palms and the limp naked body sinking into the mud. As the music, singing, and prayers increased around him, Lazarus heard in his mind the words of the Galilean: "Whoever believes in me shall have everlasting life." Did the Galilean know the meaning of the word *everlasting* that he used so often? Did he have any idea of what *everlasting* was?

As the sun set on the hill, an uproar was heard from the ramp. A hail of spears fell on the rebels, who desperately were defending their Temple amid the corpses of their friends, sons, and brothers. Lazarus, sitting on the now almost empty esplanade, leaning against the wall of the sanctuary, saw throats and breasts transfixed by darts.

Where the fortress had stood, the ground was covered with bodies. The praying had dwindled to a murmur, there was no more music and singing, but the smoke of the sacrifices still ascended into the darkening sky.

Five flaming missiles soared over the wall and crashed into the Beautiful Gate, which was still ajar. A handful of defenders fled into the Court of the Jews, beyond the Court of the Priests. From a curtain of fire a living torch ran, shrieking, with outflung arms, then collapsed on the pavement not far from Lazarus. A priest rushed to it and rolled it in a cloak.

Other defenders appeared, but they could offer no resistance. It was the end of Israel. What would be the point of his continuing to "witness" now, however reluctantly? Could one bear witness for the benefit of the dead?

There was another burst of flame, and the whole Temple seemed to ignite. Lazarus saw Romans pouring in through the Sheep Gate, now undefended. A hundred spears rained down on the courtyard, twenty Jews fell, and the last line of defense broke in three places. Then, hand-to-hand fighting. Above the crackling of the flames and the clash of swords, Lazarus could hear death rattles and the moans of the wounded and the dying.

Through the thickening smoke he saw a square of Romans advancing in serried ranks, with heavy regular tread. Behind their wooden shields and poised spears, their faces and bodies were hidden. They were like a blind inexorable machine rolling toward him.

He faced them without flinching.

"Take me back to the place you took me from," he whispered. "If you *are* Israel's Messiah, you know you have no need of me now."